TUULI CLOSED HER EYES.

Tuuli closed her eyes. She'd lost count of the days since her escape. Her muscles ached from the walking, and her skin felt raw and uncared for. Her belly growled with hunger, and she was cold.

Despite having escaped from that torturous prison, she was growing weaker.

She couldn't wait until dark to cross the meadow. And who knows what would be lurking there in the darkness?

She pulled up all the energy her body held. Tuuli surrounded herself with as strong a veil of invisibility as she could create.

Then she raced through the knee deep grass.

Halfway across she spotted it, the fog swiftly approaching her. A Fomorian.

She tried to find a burst of speed, but the fog was faster still.

It wrapped around her, squeezing, strangling.

She managed to get out a scream, knowing there was no one to hear. No one to help.

Just as her mind went to black, she heard a thundering noise.

And then consciousness was gone.

FAERIE FLIGHT

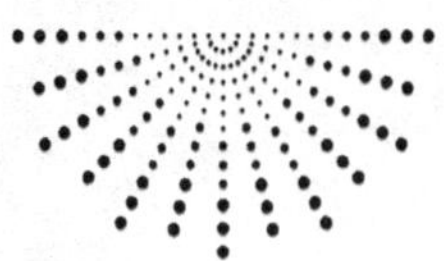

FAERIE FLIGHT

THE BONES OF THE EARTH: BOOK 4

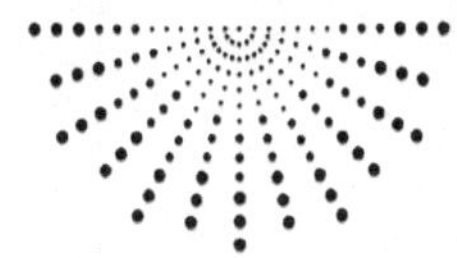

LINDA JORDAN

METAMORPHOSIS PRESS

Published by Metamorphosis Press

www.MetamorphosisPress.com

ISBN 13: 978-1946914019

For Michael & Zoe

CHAPTER 1 ~ TUULI

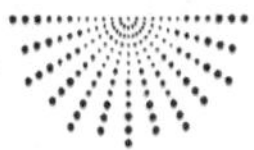

Tuuli felt the icy ground beneath her bare feet. Feet which bled from the long climb up the jagged rocks inside the tunnel. At least the cold made them numb enough she could no longer feel the pain.

Up here on the surface, the wind blew frigid air over her naked bluish skin. It roared around her like a wild beast. One that wanted to kill her. She knew danger was far from gone. It prickled up her spine, warning her to keep moving.

The cold helped bring her back to this cold body, waking her up. She squinted in the bright winter light. So intense after seasons spent in darkness, in the cave below.

The gusting wind smelled clean and fresh. When was the last time she'd breathed fresh air? She could taste ice on the wind, feel the shards of it hit her face. She stood looking into the wind. Trying to savor the cold, sharpness of it. Trying to waken her power. But it was as if she called and no one answered.

Her power felt gone, along with her wings.

Looking around, she took in the vastness of her

surroundings. Where was she? Rock, ice and sea surrounded her. She could see other piles of rocks in the distance. Across the water. None of them looked familiar. It was the dim daylight of winter. The sky above blue with clouds whipping past. No stars to be seen, nothing to recognize or help her find the way home.

Tuuli tried not to look up at the limitless sky. It was gone from her now.

Surrounding her was a vastness of gray stone and white ice and snow. The mountain was huge and made up the entire island as far as she could see.

The wind blasted across her naked body. She felt small and powerless. Not even enough strength left to warm herself in the cold. They hadn't given her food and water. Not even Fae could withstand that forever.

She dipped a handful of crusty snow and stuffed it into her mouth. It provided some water, although even that tasted salty.

She must get moving, but her heart ached from the loss. Wounds still wept on her back. The loss of her wings was the loss of herself.

She didn't have time to just stand here. They would miss her. She needed to be far away before then.

Tuuli scrambled over the sharp rocks and ice to the edge of the precipice, trying to maintain her balance. The salt in the ice burned the cuts in her feet. She felt dizzy looking down. Her mind clouded.

When in her thousand years of life had she ever felt dizzy?

Far down below the rocky cliff lay a black beach. After that she'd have to swim. Off in the distance land stood above the sea.

There. Home was in that direction. How far Tuuli didn't know. She'd just have to keep on moving till she got there.

She could make it that far.

She had to. Tears streamed down her face. If only she could still fly, it would be much easier.

If only.

The wind gusted around these heights making her naked skin feel raw. Blowing her ragged, short dark hair. Hair that had once reached her ankles. But the chill felt refreshing. Kept her awake and moving. Sylphs could handle the cold.

She climbed down a steep section of the cliff face, the jagged edges of sharp gray rock cutting the palms of her hands. Blood flowed to the surface. Tuuli ignored the pain, and the blood.

Keep moving. Just keep putting distance between yourself and the Fomorians, she told herself.

The light looked so bright after so long in the darkness. It was blinding. Even squinting, she had a hard time finding places to hang onto the cliff face.

She slipped, her breathing became ragged with panic. She'd never been afraid of falling before. Ever. But that was before. When she had wings to catch herself.

Tuuli forced herself to concentrate on each hand hold. On each spot she placed her foot. On each breath.

She gained nothing by thinking about what had been lost.

She must get away. And get help for the others.

Hours later, she stood on the narrow beach, facing the cold dark unknown of the sea. Nothing to do about it, or to do about anything that might swim beneath the surface.

If the Fomorians caught her again, they'd kill her. She might as well die trying to return to Faerie.

But she couldn't die. The others needed rescuing. There was no one else to help.

There was only her.

She must get back to Faerie and tell them.

Tuuli waded into the sea, her belly aching from hunger. When the freezing water was waist high, she began to swim. Salt burned her back. She hoped at least it cleansed the wounds.

CHAPTER 2 ~ ADAIRE

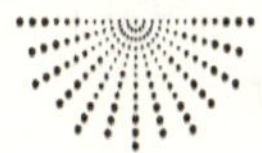

ADAIRE MOVED BENEATH THE ANCIENT ASH TREE just inside the boundary of Faerie, her loose pants and shirt, the color of green apples. She blended in with the evergreen plants of the forest. Her feet bare on the soft, moss carpet beneath the trees. Her knee-length, braided black hair held back in a leather tie.

The ground was bare of all but the evergreen ground covers. They were deep in winter, the ground frozen but no ice or snow visible. The deciduous trees and shrubs had long ago dropped their leaves, which formed a brown crust beneath her toes.

Most insects were dormant, but a few birds watched her curiously. Small goldcrests were looking for any insect hiding beneath evergreen leaves. A raven was digging beneath the frozen leaves and watching her warily. Periodically, he stopped and cawed at her.

It was too cold to smell the damp earth scent which the forest held in warmer times. The bitter oiliness of pine needles was on the air.

Many of the trees here had been burned last fall. Several would never recover. They were still receiving energy and nutrients from the healthy trees, spread through their connecting root systems. It would be a mercy to kill them. Let the other struggling trees keep their nutrients and recover more quickly. A winter storm might come through that would do just that. Or it might not and the dying trees would simply linger, weakening the others.

The tree in front of her with its furrowed gray bark had grown into a knobby trunk whose lower branches had been broken by wind or snow and removed by forest creatures or other dryads. Sections of the bark were covered with a stiff greenish-brown moss.

She touched the tree feeling its lifeblood, assessing how healthy it was. It lacked energy and vitality. It had witnessed the slaughter of its offspring. The Fomorians and dragons had battled here. Many of the other trees were badly burned. Some completely gone, others gravely damaged.

Luckily the old ash tree had escaped injury. It would survive and thrive again.

She sent healing energy to it, singing to the soul of the tree. An old song, one she'd learned as a child. Full of notes which resonated to the depths of the earth, releasing and bringing up vitality from the soil. Extra nutrients which the tree could absorb and use in this time of additional stress.

She'd gather here with the other dryads at the next waxing moon and bring the trees some extra energy and nutrients.

Her fingers caressed the deep gray grooves. The smell of damp earth surrounded her. She could feel the energy of the tree deep within, it was contemplating a slow awakening.

It would be four months, Beltane, before the tree's crinkly

green buds would open. All the other types of trees leafed out first. Ash was always the last.

In the middle of winter, spring felt a long ways away. Everyone and everything was weary from the war. And although Faerie had managed to close its borders again, and the Fomorians could no longer attack them, the monsters' presence outside the boundaries was oppressive.

Meredith and Aura's plan to make peace by giving the Fomorians mead wasn't working. The Fomorians thought the Fae were trying to poison them and threw the stoneware bottles onto the rocks, letting the honey wine pour into the earth. At least the soil appreciated the nutrients of the mead.

But nothing had really changed between the Fae and Fomorians. They were still at an impasse.

Adaire felt exhausted, as did most of Faerie.

She moved over to a burnt hazelnut tree. It was young, about ten years, but would always bear the scars. It might never grow properly on the side that was burned, but it could be saved.

Perhaps it would grow into a monument, a reminder to Faerie, of the tragedies that war brought. The loss of lives and the maiming of the survivors.

It was a vigorous tree and needed little care from her. She removed a few of the now dead branches, patted it and moved along.

The next tree was another hazelnut. This one completely dead. It had been a sapling. She cut it down with a slice of energy from her fingers, then chopped the branches into smaller pieces. Mounding them all into a neat pile for small creatures or insects to use as a home, until the wood decayed and became part of the forest floor.

Doing this work saddened her. She didn't like to choose

who would live or die. But it was part of being a dryad. More so since the war. Neither the dragons or the Fomorians likely viewed the forest as the living, breathing being she was.

The dragons were common visitors these days. She'd been told they used to live within Faerie. They probably wanted to return.

But Adaire didn't trust them. The fire elementals were problem enough in the woods, but dragons?

Could they be trusted to control themselves and not burn the entire forest down?

She sighed, wishing things were as they once had been. She didn't like this changing world. Especially after spending so long in the human world.

This part of the forest was nearly soundless. A faint rustling of branches from the breeze. The birds and animals who had lived here had fled during the battle. The trees missed their bright colors and lively movement.

It was getting late. The council had asked the dryads to meet with them tonight. She'd better begin heading back.

Tomorrow, she'd return and see what she could do for the rest of the trees.

She moved onto the road, the fastest route to the palace. Then began to run. Stretching out her long legs, it didn't take any time at all before her breathing came in gasps. Adaire slowed her pace a bit.

She was out of shape for running. Hadn't done it in far too long. There had been too much to do during the war and she hadn't taken the time to care for herself.

As she passed through the forest, the trees changed from hazel and ash to yew. Then later to pine. The scents of each type of tree filled the air. Even trees without leaves had their own particular scent. As did each different type of shrub and some perennials.

Most Fae couldn't smell them. But dryads could. The strength of a plant's scent was another marker of health.

Still, she kept on running, her feet pounding soundlessly on the stone road.

She startled a small herd of red deer, who then raced alongside her for a time. Later, a flock of goldcrests scattered as she passed.

In one section of the forest, Adaire ran through a rain shower. The cold water felt good on her now hot skin. She tilted her head up and caught raindrops in her mouth. The fresh, clean water quenched her thirst and drenched her clothes.

The sun was beginning to set when she left the forest. The palace, up on the hill, rose into view. The days were still short, dark and cold.

But spring was coming.

.

CHAPTER 3 ~ TUULI

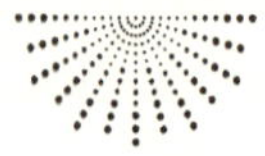

Tuuli struggled through the heavy brush. Bare of leaves, the brambles tore at her ragged skin. Old, hard thorns, on dead and fallen branches, pierced her already battered feet. But it felt safer here than being out in the open.

The land around her was grassy, rolling hills. In the folds between the hills stood trees and brambles and bushes. She had to follow the lowland here in order to stay hidden. She hadn't recovered enough of her power to use that to hide herself. Or maybe her magic would never return now that her wings were gone.

Only occasionally, did she run across a stream that smelled clean enough to drink from. She had nothing to carry water in so thirst followed her.

She'd been walking for days now. It was the middle of winter here. Nearly all the trees and bushes were bare. The days and nights were cold. Mostly, it was rainy and the clouds blocked the stars, which might have told her where she was.

She walked through human land. Could hear their cars and

planes. Smell their woodsmoke or smoke from the cars. Fae did not belong among humans. She felt small, lost and afraid.

And she could smell them. The Fomorians.

Tuuli couldn't tell if they were the ones she escaped from and they were tracking her, or if she'd just stupidly happened upon another group of them. They all smelled the same to her. A mixture of rotting flesh, fresh feces and vomit. As well as unwashed bodies.

The smell made her gag. She covered her mouth, not wanting to be heard.

Tuuli wasn't using any magic, except a small shielding spell. Trying to remain invisible.

The air felt cold and fresh, which actually felt exhilarating after so long time spent in the close, stuffy cage, deep in the earth.

She was completely disoriented. She knew Faerie lay vaguely to the south. But Tuuli had no idea where she was, or how far from Faerie.

Why couldn't she remember this land she'd once flown over?

It was as if the entire landscape had changed. How long had she been held prisoner?

She moved beneath a grove of large trees. Green moss lay like velvet there beneath the oaks. Her feet appreciated the softness.

Her back ached and felt hot. She knew that meant there was an infection, but there was nothing she could do about it at the moment. The crusty wounds had scarred over.

Still, she dreamed about flying. Every single night.

Tuuli tried not to think about the previous night's dreams, instead concentrating on her surroundings. Hazelnut. Oak. Ash. Yew.

She'd foraged in the hedgerows and found a few bilberries from the previous summer, now shriveled and dried. And some very tart rose hips. None of those had done much to satisfy her grumbling stomach.

Mostly she just kept walking. Trying to get as far as possible from her prison.

One step. Then another. Moving closer to Faerie.

Then the woodland ended. She had no choice but to cross the open meadow to the next group of trees.

She stood staring, looking for anything that might cause her trouble. She saw only a flock of ravens perched in the burnt-looking trees across the grassy expanse.

Tuuli closed her eyes. She'd lost count of the days since her escape. Her muscles ached from the walking, and her skin felt raw and uncared for. Her belly growled with hunger, and she was cold.

Despite having escaped from that torturous prison, she was growing weaker.

She couldn't wait until dark to cross the meadow. And who knows what would be lurking there in the darkness?

She pulled up all the energy her body held. Tuuli surrounded herself with as strong a veil of invisibility as she could create.

Then she raced through the knee deep grass.

Halfway across she spotted it, the fog swiftly approaching her. A Fomorian.

She tried to find a burst of speed, but the fog was faster still.

It wrapped around her, squeezing, strangling.

She managed to get out a scream, knowing there was no one to hear. No one to help.

Just as her mind went to black, she heard a thundering noise.

And then consciousness was gone.

CHAPTER 4 ~ ADAIRE

ADAIRE RAN UP THE CARVED, WHITE, STONE STAIRS to the palace, taking two at a time. The building had shifted again, taking the form of a forest of tall, pine trees with a watertight canopy. They must have been a hundred feet tall, thick and bushy. Ravens, and crows, as well as many smaller birds flitted between the branches.

It was slightly warmer here in the center of Faerie. Although, a narrow plume of light gray smoke rose up through the center of the trees. The fire would be in the throne room, warming those inside.

Strung between the trees were brilliant tapestries woven with brightly colored threads. The glimmer of gold flashed in the waning sunlight. She'd never seen them here before. The tapestries were massive. Who had woven them and how long had it taken? She felt them calling to her, making her want to look at them more closely. Powerful magic.

She felt sure if she were to examine all the scenes, the history of Faerie would be laid out among them.

Wishing she had time to linger and look at the tapestries,

Adaire reached the top of the stairs and bent over, breathing hard.

Up here, on the top of the hill, she could see for miles all around. The wind brought the scent of the sea to her. And a chill along with it.

She shivered, longing for spring and new growth. She was tired of the cold, but it was still winter, the season of death. She should have gone into a tree for the winter.

Adaire turned and went inside the great carved wooden doors of the palace. Inside the structure hadn't changed. The massive stone pillars and carved wooden walls looked the same.

In the throne room, off to the left, sat the Council of Elders. The six Luminaries. Faerie's ruling body. They each sat on their own throne which represented the element they were most at home in. Although, like the palace, those thrones had changed over time.

Meredith, protector of the sea, had a throne made of a sea-green colored stone which was draped with kelp and shells. There were fish and other sea creatures elaborately carved onto it. The stone had channels carved into it which funneled the water that seeped from her skin (as happened to water elementals) down to the earth below.

Aura's throne was made of delicate branches and veils of silver, woven throughout the branches. One of two remaining sylphs in Faerie, she represented the air elementals.

The throne of Alana was made of chiseled rock, to represent the stone people. The angular rock looked hard and uncomfortable to Adaire, but seemed to suit the earth elder.

Brian's throne was made of wood, twisted reeds, and grasses. It looked as wild and tangled as his hair. He was another earth elder.

A living tree formed Ogden's throne. The now bare-branched oak rose up, one massive trunk, to form part of the support for the palace. The other trunk curled around and formed the seat for him. He was Adaire's mentor, another earth elder and a dryad.

Conley's throne was created from metals: silver, gold and black metal, forming the shape of flames for the fire elemental.

The elders looked relaxed. Carrying on conversation while waiting for everyone to appear.

Adaire nodded at them and took a seat in the circle. One of the palace Fae came over to her and offered a tray of beverages. Adaire took a mug of fresh clean water. She sipped it, feeling the cool water slide down her throat and into her empty belly. She hadn't eaten in a day or two, so intent on healing the forest.

She listened to the elders discuss whether to keep trying to give the Fomorians mead.

"They will just destroy it, as they have with all the other attempts," said Conley.

"So, we should just give up," said Meredith, a sarcastic tinge to her voice.

Off to the side, one of the yellow and orange scaled fire Fae stoked a fire which kept the chill off the large room. A metal funnel hanging down from the ceiling sucked the smoke up and out of the room. Mostly. There were four fire pits in the throne room. This was the only one currently lit.

The wind off the sea had cooled her, and the fire felt comforting.

Ogden, the dryad, nodded to Adaire. She returned his greeting, holding her middle three fingers up, their sacred symbol of the forest. He repeated her gesture.

Another palace Fae brought a silver platter of freshly baked bread around to everyone. Adaire took a slice, the bread was filled with hazelnuts and dried berries. She nibbled on it, appreciating the sweet heartiness. About the time she finished the bread, the other dryads had trickled in and taken seats.

Meredith stood to speak.

She was a Water elder. One of the few left.

Water Fae often had squishy looking bodies which belied their massive strength. Their hair often looked like a living creature, like sea anemone's arms. Meredith was no exception. Her skin was a sea green color and her waist length hair wild and unruly. She wore a long-sleeved, royal blue blouse and skirt made of oilcloth. In the summer water spirits normally went naked, as did many of the other Fae, but in the winter many Fae wore clothing for the extra warmth.

"Good evening. Thank you for coming. We welcome all of you here. I'll begin. Since Faerie has been closed everything has been moving along smoothly. The lake has frozen again, so most of the water elementals are very quiet and beneath the water. This is typically the season where we retreat and rest. Only Dylan, a few others, and I, are above water at this time. Dylan's been busy painting and trying to decide whether to leave Faerie with Solange or stay here with her. That's all I have to say right now. Aura, you're next.

Meredith sat down and Aura stood.

The Air elder was slight and looked like the wind could blow her away. She had transparent wings and ankle-length, silver hair, woven through with blue ribbons and braids. She wore a diaphanous blue, purple and pink robe, more for color than for modestly or warmth.

She smiled and looked at every single Fae. Air spirits, sylphs especially, were known for their graciousness.

"I have been having disturbing dreams of late. Dreams of

the missing sylphs. Of torture and death. But also of running and swimming. I believe at least one of the sylphs has escaped. We can only hope they make it back here and tell us where the others are hidden. Until the Fomorians are taken care of, we cannot go out searching for them. It would be foolish to risk the lives of more Fae without knowing more than we do."

She bowed and turned to Ogden, gesturing for him to speak.

Ogden was an oak dryad, an Earth elder.

He stood, tall and slender. His skin was gnarled as an old oak, his beard wispy like dried moss.

"Our forests have been badly damaged in this war. We've lost some of the ancients. But the forests will recover with time. Unlike other elementals, we've lost few dryads. There are enough of us to do the work. Do you have anything to add Adaire?"

She stood and said, "The Northern forest is very damaged. But the trees left will recover, if they're given care. They feel safer now that the boundaries are back up. But the dragons..."

"Yes," said Ogden. "I'd like to address that. The dragons make the trees uneasy. Everything is so easily burned."

Meredith said, "I will speak to the dragons. It will take time for Faerie to get used to dragons being present again and it will also take time for dragons to get used to taking care of other living things. But they understand it is part of our bargain in letting them return."

Adaire shivered and sat down. Would she ever get used to dragons in Faerie? Probably not. She'd grown up with the horror stories.

Ogden sat down and waved at Alana.

Alana stood. She was a stooped Earth elder, one of the stone Fae. Her skin was gray and hard looking, the bones in her face were chiseled angles. Alana's steely gray eyes told you that she missed nothing. She wore no clothes, and no ornamentation in her waist-length, gray hair. Her body as angular as her face.

"We stone Fae have had heavy losses during this war. The Fomorians have devastated our numbers. It will be many millennia before our element is healthy again. I understand this war was not entered into lightly, but I don't believe I will ever again agree to such an act. The devastation has been overwhelming for all of us. We mourn deeply."

She sat and gestured to Brian, a tall Earth elder.

"I have nothing to add," he said, running a hand through his long, grassy hair. He also wore no clothes or ornamentation.

Conley stood. He was a Fire elder. Like most older fire Fae, his skin was scaled over the top of the head, back, chest and arms in yellow, orange and red. He wore a metal skirt of armor, which had become popular among the fire Fae during this war. It reminded Adaire of human, Roman armor.

He said, "We fire Fae have also been devastated during this war. In hindsight, it was a mistake. We thought we could have an effect on the Fomorians. Clearly, we were wrong. We will probably recover more quickly than you other elementals. It is the way of fire. I believe we must continue to search for a way to defeat them. I have a difficult time believing the Fomorians will ever live peaceably with us. I may be wrong, but I don't think we can ever let our guard down with them."

Conley sat down and at the moment the palace shook as if an earthquake was happening.

"Dragon," said Meredith.

Everyone rushed for the palace entrance. Eager for any news.

Adaire stayed towards the back of the crowd.

Outside, the air had grown even cooler and dusk filled the sky. The palace lit the torches out in front and flames roared in the fire pit on the landing.

Beside it, stood a huge black dragon.

He bowed, and said, "My apologies for the unannounced interruption. I found this Fae being attacked by a Fomorian. The Fog. I rescued her, but I do not know if I was quick enough."

At his front feet lay an unconscious Fae.

Aura screamed and fainted at the sight of the Fae.

Ogden caught her, before she hit the ground. He lifted her and carried her back inside.

Brian lifted the unconscious Fae and took her inside.

Adaire watched Meredith move closer to the dragon.

"Thank you, what you did was right. We will try to revive her."

"I must return to the battle," said the black dragon.

Meredith nodded and moved away from the dragon, towards the walls of the palace.

The dragon shot straight up into the air and the blast of wind that followed knocked Adaire to the ground.

Meredith helped her up and said, "They always do that. It's best to stand in the shelter of the palace."

Adaire followed her into the palace, rubbing the sore spot on her hip, where she'd fallen hard.

The Fae had been laid out on a table and the healers called. Aura was standing beside her, weeping.

Adaire stared at them, trying to make sense of it all. It was as if Aura knew the unconscious Fae. No one else seemed to. Which would make the Fae an air spirit. A sylph.

But she had no wings.

An earth healer came and stood on one end of the table. Meredith took a place on the other end. Aura was on one side and Conley on the other side.

They began an ancient chant in the old language. Everyone in the room formed a circle around the healers. They extended their hands to the side, fingertips touching. Adaire could feel the flow of energy grow stronger and then everyone, pushed it forward for the healers to access.

The energy began to glow and passed through the healers, forming a spinning circle over the injured Fae.

Adaire watched as the elders tempered the energy to make it balanced. More water and air were added, the earth and fire energy damped down a bit. When the balance was struck, the energy was poured into the unconscious Fae, who absorbed it. She began to glow again.

All Fae had a glow about them, an aura, which was unlike that of humans or any other creature. They lost that glow when near death or dead. The Council had confirmed that it was a Fae's glow which enabled the Fomorians to find them.

The elders kept pouring energy into the injured Fae, until she opened her eyes. Then they dropped their arms as did everyone else. Still the energy hummed around the room for some time, making everyone appear brighter and more vital.

Adaire felt enlivened, being at a healing healed everyone.

The air spirit sat up and looked around. It was then that Adaire saw what the problem was.

On the sylph's back were two red wounds where her wings had been.

She turned away, it was painful to even look at, let alone think about what had been done to the sylph.

CHAPTER 5 ~ TUULI

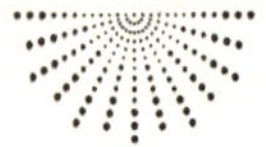

Tuuli felt warm again. And safe, somehow.

When had she last felt safe?

She didn't want to open her eyes. Didn't want to know where she was. Not really.

She felt the hum of magic around her.

That made Tuuli open her eyes. Far above hung a carved wooden ceiling. Closer, hovered a ring of power, such as she'd only seen once. During a healing.

She felt alive again.

It took her a few minutes before it came to her that the ring of power had been made to heal her. It was so bright she couldn't see the faces behind it. But she felt the presence of air energy, and sighed with relief.

She was in a building. That much was clear. And the carved ceiling was ornate. The golden wood beams were graceful and carved. Was she in Faerie?

Tuuli had seen so little of the world that she wouldn't know if this was a human building or not. And she'd only glimpsed humans, staying far away from them. Faerie had been closed when she was just born. And it had only just opened after the young fire Fae took power. Then she'd been taken by the Fomorians.

She shuddered and sat up. Determined to face whatever was happening.

The healers put their arms down and the ring of power dissipated.

She looked around, searching for a familiar face.

Aura.

The elder reached out to hold her and Tuuli buried her face in Aura's soft long hair, sobbing.

Aura held and rocked her.

Finally, Tuuli remembered.

"I have to tell you. The others. They are still prisoners. You must rescue them before they are all killed. Or worse."

"It is all right, dear child. Where are they?" asked Aura.

Tuuli sent a message with her mind, showing the path she'd taken from her prison. But walking was different from flying. She couldn't really show Aura.

Aura said, "Is there a map anywhere?"

"I'll go down to the library and get one," said a water elder, who Tuuli didn't recognize. "Any particular place?"

"North. North and east, I think," said Aura.

Aura held her. And eventually looked at her back.

The sorrow in the ancient sylph's eyes was almost unbearable for Tuuli to look at.

An earth Fae brought Tuuli a stoneware mug of warm fragrant broth. Which she took gratefully and drank, although her hands shook. Another earth Fae, a dryad, helped her steady the heavy mug.

The broth had bits of salty meat in it. And herbs she couldn't place. It was warming and satisfying. It helped fill in the empty places in her belly.

When she was finished the earth Fae who'd brought it, took the mug away.

"I do not understand how I got here," said Tuuli. "I was crossing a meadow. I smelled Fomorians, and was invisible. Then halfway across the meadow, a Fomorian appeared. Fog."

"Cethlenn," said Aura.

"And the monster smothered me, trying to strangle me. Everything went dark. And then I woke up here."

"The dragon must have rescued you then," said Aura.

"Dragon?" asked Tuuli. Her chest tightened. Everyone knew dragons tried to kill Fae.

"The dragons are our allies. It appears they were long ago, as well," said Aura.

Tuuli shook her head. Nothing made sense anymore. The world had turned upside down.

The water Fae returned with a paper and laid it out on the table with gloved hands.

Aura looked at it and asked, "Is this the way you came from?"

Tuuli looked at it. She'd never seen a map before, but had tried to envision the land as if flying above it, while she'd been walking. She'd never walked so much in her life.

"I suppose the sizes of the sea and land look right. This is where I was imprisoned. In a cave, deep in the Earth," she said, pointing to a large island.

"Were there many Fomorians near?" asked the Water elder.

"When I escaped there was just the one, that I saw. The wind. There were more earlier. When we were captured."

"And what were you imprisoned in?" the Water elder asked.

Tuuli tried to talk, but she began to shake and sob. She couldn't talk. The memory of the pain was just too much.

Then everything grew dark again.

CHAPTER 6 ~ ADAIRE

ADAIRE WATCHED THE INJURED SYLPH WITH GRIEF. She could feel her loss. It was as tangible as the mug Adaire helped her hold.

The wounds on her back were terrible. They oozed and smelled, not yet healed.

But worse were the internal wounds, Adaire knew.

She'd watched her friend Skye, another sylph, struggle with not being able to fly because it wasn't safe. It had been so painful for her.

To have one's wings ripped off, to lose that ability forever, must be a thousand times worse.

It would be like Adaire never being able to speak with her beloved trees again.

Then all of a sudden, the sylph had blacked out.

Adaire caught her before she fell onto her injured back.

The earth healer, Willow said, "We must clean and treat her wounds."

Aura said, "Of course. Why don't you take her upstairs to a room and get started. We need to finish here, and then I'll be up. Would you go with her Adaire? Keep her company if she wakes again. Her name is Tuuli. I think you know, more than most, what might comfort her."

"I'd be honored," said Adaire.

Adaire had been held prisoner by the Fomorians as well. Before Tuuli had. With Egan, Meredith, Skye, Dylan, Lynette, Pearce, and Glenna. They'd all managed to escape and return to Faerie.

It had been awful. Days and nights filled with the pain of being trapped in a cold metal box. The cold metal had jabbed itself into her body, mind and soul.

Adaire tried to push the memories away.

Afterwards Glenna had vanished into her valley in Faerie and Lynette into a small lake. They'd both been so traumatized from the imprisonment that they refused to come out of their homes at all.

The others had all felt stronger than before their capture. And Egan had even become Luminary and taken over Faerie.

Even Adaire felt more powerful. More able to heal the forest.

She helped the other earth Fae carry Tuuli up to the second floor of the palace. The sylph didn't weigh much. The palace opened a door at their approach, and they walked into an airy blue and white room with gauzy fabric over the walls.

"Let us lie her on her front," said Willow.

They turned her over and lay Tuuli face down on the bed. Adaire positioned her head sideways, so the sylph could breathe freely.

"I need a bowl of water and a soft cloth," said Willow.

Adaire looked around, and found both on a table.

She brought them to the healer, who used them to clean Tuuli's wounds.

Another healer, Rush, came in the door. She carried a tray with a bowl of steaming brown paste and a bundle of white fabric.

After Tuuli's wounds were cleaned, the first healer spread the thick paste over the wounds, then they held her up and wrapped the fabric over her shoulders and back. They did the same with her cut feet.

"Do not let her remove these, no matter how much they itch. We will take them off tomorrow and she can bathe at the same time. She may or may not need to put more herbs on her back. We will have to wait and see," said Willow.

"I'll make sure she leaves them alone, thank you."

"You are very welcome. It is a terrible thing that was done to her," said Rush.

The two healers took their supplies and returned to the kitchen, leaving Adaire alone with Tuuli.

She looked at the pale sylph lying on the bed and covered her with a light blanket.

There were dark hollows beneath the air spirit's eyes. Adaire had never seen that in Fae, although it was common enough in humans.

She poured herself a glass of water from a pitcher and drank the room temperature liquid, rolling it around in her mouth. Once again she realized how wonderful the water in Faerie was. The life blood.

Adaire looked out the window. This room looked out over the front courtyard, where the now empty vault stood. Fae had been trying for a season now to get it cleaned. They used all manner of concoctions to try to clean it.

After a couple seasons of holding Fomorians prisoner, Adaire didn't think it would ever be clean again. Much of the contents had been completely ruined, Faerie's treasures.

Carved furniture broken and paintings defecated on. The Fomorians were filth.

There had been nothing to do to salvage so much. They'd had to be burned, their energy set free.

Only the metal items had survived the abuse mostly unscathed. And the sacred four: the spear of Lugh, the sword of Nuada, the cauldron of Dagda, the stone of Fal. It seemed nothing could harm items carrying such powerful magic.

So the empty vault had been left open to the air in hopes that time and the elements could clean it.

Adaire heard a noise behind her and she turned.

Tuuli was sitting up.

"Oh, hello," said Adaire.

"Where am I?" asked the sylph, her eyes wide.

"You're safe. In Faerie. In the palace."

"How did I get here?"

"A dragon brought you."

"A dragon." The look on Tuuli's face said she didn't believe Adaire.

"A dragon. You were attacked in the meadow just outside of Faerie. By a Fomorian, the fog. One of the dragons attacked the Fomorian and brought you here."

Tuuli shook her head, as if to clear it and asked, "Who are you?"

"I'm Adaire. Aura asked me to stay with you until she's finished with the Council."

"The Council."

"Faerie's now ruled by a Council of Luminaries. All elders."

"How long have I been gone?" asked Tuuli.

"When were you taken?"

"Just after the boundaries of Faerie fell. After the Fomorians were imprisoned. I flew with all the other sylphs. The palace was too hot from the new Luminary. The fire Fae. So we flew out past where the boundaries had been. To see how the world had changed. Some of them had seen it millennia ago, before Faerie was closed. Then we were taken, one after another."

Tuuli looked down at her hands.

"Are you all right?" asked Adaire, knowing it was a stupid question.

"I do not think I will ever be all right again," said Tuuli. "I wish I had never left Faerie."

Adaire said nothing. There was nothing she could say.

They sat in silence for a time. Finally, Tuuli got out of the bed and looked around the room. She stared out the window, presumably at the vault. Adaire saw that she avoided looking up at the sky.

Tuuli limped towards a closet and pulled out a blue silky robe. She put it on over her bandages. And slipped on a pair of soft knitted slippers over the bandages on her feet.

"I suppose I have to stay up here," said Tuuli.

"This is where Aura will come looking for you," said Adaire.

"Why are you here? I do not mean to be rude, but you are an earth spirit."

"You, Aura, and Skye are the only air spirits around. And Skye isn't in Faerie right now."

"They took everyone else?"

"Yes."

Tuuli sank into a cushioned chair.

"And I'm here because I was captured by the Fomorians. And escaped. I believe Aura thought that might comfort you somehow."

Tuuli stared at her with those innocent blue eyes, filled with sadness and wonder.

"What happened?"

"I was one of the Fae who left Faerie when it was closed millennia ago. For a very long time I lived in the forests, healing trees. Then I began to understand that many humans had come unmoored from their connection to the Earth. So I lived among them, trying to teach them where I could. Helping them to heal the little patches of soil they called home. That's what I was doing when I left my human body behind for an evening. To walk among the trees as myself. A dryad. The Fomorians caught me then. Are you sure you want to hear this?"

Tuuli nodded.

"I was imprisoned in a cold metal box with Skye, Egan, and Dylan. In the next cell were Meredith, Glenna, Pearce, and Lynette. Through the use of all our powers we managed to weaken the boxes and make holes in them. Then we escaped and made our way back to Faerie to warn them. There must have been a hundred Fae in the place where the Fomorians held us. All the rest had died."

Tuuli had her hand over her mouth, and tears ran down her cheeks.

Adaire came and sat on a chair across from her, brushing the hot liquid away.

"That is awful. What happened when you got back to Faerie?"

"We found Varion, the Luminary, doing nothing. He barely cared, although Meredith was his sister. Egan took over and you know the rest."

"Except that I do not. I have been gone for so long."

"There was a war. It's still happening. But nothing we've done seems to be able to affect the Fomorians for long. Even the dragons can't seem to kill them. So we opened the vault, releasing Balor and his followers. We tricked them into moving outside the boundaries of Faerie and then closed the boundaries again. Sealing the edges better this time."

"Will they send someone to rescue the other sylphs?"

"I think they must. Faerie is sorely in need of air spirits."

Tuuli nodded.

The door opened and Aura came into the room. She sat in a chair near Tuuli and asked, "How are you?"

"I am alive," said Tuuli.

"We will send a group of stone and fire Fae to rescue the others. Let us hope they succeed."

"How will they cross the water?" asked Adaire.

"Dragons. They have gone to ask the dragons to fly them there."

"And the dragons will help?" asked Tuuli.

"Yes, they will," said Aura. "Now, the healers tell me that your wounds are infected. You must leave the bandages on and let the herbs do their work. A healer will come tomorrow to remove the bandages and help you bathe. Then we will see how you are healing."

Tuuli looked down.

"Tell me what happened," said Aura.

It was not a question, Adaire noticed.

Tuuli said, "We went exploring. After the boundaries of Faerie had fallen and the Fomorians imprisoned. All of us. Skeeter wanted to make sure no Fomorians escaped. That all of them had been trapped in the vault. So we split off into four different groups, flying in all directions. Our group flew north. We did not see any Fomorians, but they saw us. One moment I was flying with the others, the next I was trapped in a cold steel box. I hit the wall inside the box and the cold steel went right through me. I felt completely helpless."

She sat shuddering on the chair.

Adaire got up and poured a drink of water for the sylph, handing it to her.

"Thank you," Tuuli said.

"Do you want to tell me more?" asked Aura.

"Will it do any good?" asked Tuuli. "It will not bring my wings back."

"Why did they take your wings. I do not understand."

"They did not say. I think they just wanted to hurt me. I know they hurt the others too. I could hear their screams sometimes," she said.

The sylph looked paler than ever with dark circles beneath her hollowed out eyes in contrast to her light skin.

"Do you need something to eat?" asked Adaire.

"I am hungry," Tuuli said. "Thank you."

Adaire left the room, closing the door quietly.

She felt cold. Pushing the sylph's story out of her mind, she padded quickly down the cool stone stairs in her bare feet and went towards the back of the palace. Where she supposed the kitchen lay.

After a couple of wrong turns, she found it.

There were six earth Fae working at various jobs. Stirring giant pots of steaming liquid, chopping vegetables, washing fruit and kneading bread. The kitchen felt warm and smelled delicious.

"What can I help you with?" asked a tall, fully clothed Fae whose long and braided, green hair was tied in a bundle at her back.

"Tuuli, the injured sylph is very hungry. I was wondering if I could get something to bring up to her."

"Of course," said the Fae. "How about some beef and barley soup? It has probably been some time since she ate a good meal. It will not be good to make her sick from eating too much."

"I think you're right."

The Fae ladled up a bowl of soup and put on a tray. It was then that Adaire realized the soup was the source of that delicious smell. Her stomach growled loudly.

"I heard that," said the Fae. "I better fill another bowl."

And she did. Then put a plate of sliced walnut bread and a bowl with butter on the tray.

"Aura is up there too, is she not?"

Adaire nodded.

In the end, she carried up a bowl for everyone, plus bread and butter, and baked pears with a wine sauce for dessert.

When Adaire entered Tuuli's room, the palace created a small round table, and made three chairs appear. Adaire set the tray down in the center of the table. The three of them pulled up the chairs and began to eat.

The barley made the soup hearty. The beef fell apart in her mouth as she began to chew, releasing its strong flavor. Adaire tasted oregano, onion, and carrots.

The bread was chewy and robust, sprinkled with bits of walnuts that melded with the richness of the butter.

It was a wonderful meal. Adaire stared at the baked pear for a long time before deciding to eat it, even though she was already full.

It tasted of cinnamon and wine. The pear melted in her mouth.

Not a word was spoken during the meal and afterwards the three of them sat in silence.

The cold and darkness of the world outside was made warm by candle sconces on the wall, which the palace lit. A warm fire in the fireplace roared and even Adaire felt glad of the warmth.

She hadn't felt a cold winter in a very long time, having spent the last several years in Seattle.

Outside it was bitter cold. Faerie of old had somehow moderated the temperature so that it remained summer year round. Either the Council of Luminaries had chosen not to do so, or it hadn't occurred to them.

After the meal Aura said, "I must return downstairs. There is much to do."

"I will stay," said Adaire.

Aura swept out of the room with the grace that only sylphs have. In contrast Adaire felt clumsy.

She stacked the dishes back on the tray and took them down to the kitchen. When she returned to Tuuli's room, the sylph was already asleep in the bed.

Adaire curled up on a loveseat. The palace stretched it out into another bed and spread a warm blanket over her. It extinguished the candles, but left the fire burning all night, taking the chill off the room.

CHAPTER 7 ~ TUULI

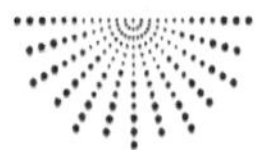

TUULI WOKE THE NEXT MORNING HER BACK ACHING. She got up and stretched. The dryad was still sleeping.

The sun was almost rising and there was enough dim light to shine through the gauzy curtained windows illuminating the room with a warm glow. The walls were covered with the same fabric, giving the place a cloud-like feel.

She wished the healers would come, her back itched as well as ached. And all she could smell were the herbs they must have used. The scent was stagnant and rotting. But it could have been just her. She couldn't remember the last time she'd been able to clean herself.

Tuuli stood by the window, looking through the sheer white fabric. It had snowed overnight and the land looked peaceful and pristine. Last winter at this time she had been able to fly around Faerie. Not outside of it, because Faerie had still been closed. But Faerie had always held enough wonders for her to see.

What would she do now? Now that she was back in Faerie. With no wings. She really had no place here. Nothing to do.

The imprisonment of the other sylphs weighed on her.

She needed to help them. But how?

She'd never catch up to the rescuers on foot. And even if she could convince a horse to go out in the middle of winter on such a venture, it couldn't swim the sea.

The stone and fire Fae had taken dragons.

Would a dragon carry her back to the cave?

If she went back there must be something she could do to help the other sylphs escape.

But she was afraid.

And still injured.

Adaire rustled beneath her blanket and sat up, a strange look on her face as if she was disoriented. Trying to figure out where she was and how she got there.

"Good morning," said Tuuli.

"Good morning. Is it morning yet?"

"The sun will rise shortly. But it is morning. The warblers and the wrens have begun to sing. And there is snow."

Adaire groaned.

"What is wrong with snow."

"I know it's the way of things, but it breaks branches off the older trees. Ones who can no longer hold themselves up. And there are so many trees struggling this season. Otherwise it would be fine to let them drop off, but so many of the trees here are damaged and compromised."

"Why?"

"Because of the war. So many got burned or blasted by the Fomorians."

"What do you know about the dragons?"

"Not very much. They came in the late fall, I think. I'm not really sure. I was out in the forests. Egan called them. Requested their help in killing the Fomorians. They asked to be let back into Faerie. To be taught Fae magic. And one of the elders, Meredith I think, found records of Faerie's past. The dragons used to be part of Faerie. But they committed a horrendous crime and were banished. By one of the ancient Luminaries. I guess the Council decided they'd been punished long enough. So they agreed to teach the dragons. And apparently they've found their old weirs, which are covered in stunning paintings done by the dragons. At least that's what I've heard."

"That is a lot," said Tuuli. "Do you know where to find them? Or contact them?"

"No, but Dylan does. He's been going to their old weirs and studying the paintings. Why?"

"I wish to thank the dragon who saved me."

"You're not afraid of them?" asked Adaire.

"Yes. But I still owe them thanks. Perhaps speaking to one will help ease my fear."

She couldn't tell Adaire why she really wanted to speak to a dragon. Could she? Tuuli didn't know how far to trust the dryad.

"You're so brave."

"You mean I am brave for a sylph?"

Sylphs were known for their speed at flying from a fight.

"No, I mean you're brave. The dragons terrify me."

"Well, the Fomorians terrify me more."

Adaire said, "I'm not afraid of the Fomorians killing me. Death doesn't frighten me. But being imprisoned again and tortured, I am afraid of that. The dragons terrify me more, though. I was there when they killed so many of us. Their fire. …"

"That makes sense. Fire, trees burning. But sylphs do not normally have as much of a problem with fire."

"That's true. When Egan took over as Luminary, Skye was the only one who could bear to be around him."

"I would like to meet her. She left Faerie before I was born."

"I'm sure she'll return. Or perhaps we'll find a solution to the Fomorians and Faerie will be opened again. Then you could go see her."

"But I can not fly," said Tuuli.

"Humans have buses, trains and boats. That's how those of us who don't have wings get around. And walking, of course."

Tuuli had no interest in using human transportation. She just wanted to fly again. To be whole.

There was a knock at the door and Willow entered.

"I have come to clean your back again," she said. "You are looking much better this morning. I think it is time for a bath for you."

Adaire asked, "Do you need my help?"

"No dear. I think we are just fine."

"I'll go downstairs and get some breakfast. I'll meet you down there, Tuuli. Introduce you to Dylan."

"All right."

Adaire closed the door behind her.

Willow drew back a curtain in one corner of the room. There sat a white and blue tiled bathing pool inset into the floor. Warm clean water flowed into it and older water was drained out. Willow tossed several handfuls of herbs into the water. Tuuli supposed they were to help heal her back.

The healer unwrapped the bandages from Tuuli. She could feel the cool air on her skin. It was still wet from the herb mixture.

"Get into the pool and soak for a bit. Then we'll see how your wounds look."

Tuuli stepped into the warm water. It felt wonderful. She

hadn't had a bath since before she'd been captured. Her skin felt raw and broken in so many places. And she stank.

As she soaked the grease and grime began to come off. Willow waded in with her, cleaned her short hair and began to brush the tangles out. Her hair would grow back, but it would take a very long time for it to reach her ankles. Which was where it had been before the Fomorian chopped it off with his sword. Just before he sliced off her wings.

"I am sorry," said Willow. "I did not mean to hurt you."

"You did not. I was just remembering."

Tuuli picked up a sponge, which she knew had been collected by water Fae, and scrubbed her hands. It would take many such baths to get all the dirt from beneath her fingernails. Her feet she had to go slower with. There were so many cuts. Her feet hadn't been tough after being kept in a cage. She'd grown unused to walking. And with wings, she hadn't walked that often. She supposed her feet were harder now, from days and days of walking.

After a time Willow said, "Rinse off and we'll dry your back. Take a look at the wounds.

Tuuli finished cleaning herself and rinsed off. Then stood, water dripping off her. She stepped out of the pool, which was now filled with muddy water. It would clean itself.

Willow wrapped a towel around her and patted her back carefully, drying it. Once Tuuli was dried off, Willow removed the towel and examined her back.

"The infection is gone and your wounds are healing nicely. I believe you can go without bandages, but be careful not to scrape the wounds. With luck, they will stay closed and continue to heal. I will put some herbal oil on them that will speed up the healing."

Tuuli felt Willow gently rub oil onto her back.

"I have some cuts on my feet. From running. I think the cuts on my hands are mostly healed."

Willow examined them and rubbed oil on her feet and hands. Then went to cabinet and opened the doors. From a shelf, she got a pair of soft, sky blue socks. She slipped them over Tuuli's feet.

"Put some shoes on over these for today. I will leave the oil here for you. Rub some oil on your feet and hands tonight and tomorrow morning. And ask Adaire to put some on your back as well. That should take care of any cuts. If you have any problems, let me know," said Willow, bowing and walking towards the door.

"What is in the oil?"

Willow smiled, "Secret healer's recipe."

With that she was gone.

Tuuli went to the cupboard and found soft blue pants and a loose shirt in the same color as the socks. She slipped them on. Beside the cabinet was a pair of tan leather shoes which she pulled on and tied.

Her back, feet and hands felt much better just with the cleaning and the oil. She went downstairs and into the throne room.

It had changed since she'd last been here. Under Egan, the throne room had been all stones and metals. With fire everywhere.

Now it had the beautiful carved wood ceiling Tuuli had seen when she'd woken after the dragon brought her. Wooden tables and benches were clustered together in different parts of the room, most of them empty.

There was only one burning fire pit. The smoke vented upwards, unlike during Egan's dominion, where the room seemed to have been filled with smoke.

The walls were made of more carved wood, some of the panels draped with complex tapestries. Towards the far end of the room six elaborate chairs, or thrones, formed a half circle, each of the chairs different and seeming to represent the elements of its occupant.

They must be the Council of Luminaries. Aura sat in one of the chairs.

Most Fae were sitting at the nearest grouping of tables and benches, eating breakfast. The room was more crowded than it had been last night.

She found Adaire sitting at a table across from a water Fae, who must be Dylan.

He had pale green skin and stringy green hair, almost like a water grass. He looked muscular. Water Fae were often very strong. He wore oilcloth clothes, which was common for water Fae, as it repelled the water they sloughed off.

Surprisingly, he sat next to a human woman.

A human. In Faerie. Things *had* changed.

Tuuli slid onto the smooth bench next to Adaire.

"You're looking perkier," said Adaire.

"It has been so long since I have had a bath. It felt wonderful."

"Tuuli, this is Dylan, one of the elders of the Water Fae, and Solange, his partner."

"Hello," she said, bowing her head.

Human and Fae partners. That was strange, although not completely unknown.

"Hello," said both Dylan and Solange, returning her bow.

Tuuli poured a mug of spicy tea for herself from a teapot and stared at the platters of food. There were eggs cooked with vegetables and herbs. Slices of bacon from one of Faerie's farms. And freshly baked scones with dried wild raspberries.

Finally, she dished up some food and took a bite of the crispy bacon. The smoky flavor filled her mouth.

She looked at Solange who was staring at her. The woman had shoulder length brown hair and looked unremarkable, other than being human and in Faerie.

"You're a human. Why are your here in Faerie?" Tuuli asked, hoping she wasn't being insulting.

"I wandered in one day and met Dylan. I left a couple of times, but always came back. This time I came back for good," the woman said, leaning against Dylan and hugging his arm.

He smiled at Solange.

She looked completely lost in his spell. It happened with humans sometimes. Fae burned so brightly that humans came to them. Like moths to a flame.

Adaire said to Dylan, "Tuuli wants to speak with the dragons."

Dylan spoke while chewing, like he was in a hurry to finish his food and run off somewhere.

"That's easy enough. Spike is coming this morning. You can talk to him."

"But she wants to thank the dragon who rescued her."

Dylan said, "The dragons are all connected. To speak to one of them is to speak to all."

"Then that means the dragons here can tell us where the ones searching for the sylphs are at right now?" asked Tuuli.

This might put a crimp in her plan. If she was trying to convince a dragon to take her to the cave, it might tell the others. Who might tell Aura.

Tuuli was certain Aura would not let her leave Faerie.

"In theory," said Dylan. "Although there might be a distance problem. I don't know. We can ask Spike when he comes. He's taking me to the dragon caves again."

"Spike. That's an unusual name," said Adaire.

"The black dragons didn't have names until recently. It was a black dragon who committed the crime that got all the dragons banned from Faerie. Until Meredith spoke to them, all black dragons were seen by the others as lesser dragons," said Dylan.

"What did Meredith say to them that changed them? And who is Meredith? She must be formidable."

Dylan said, "Meredith is the Water elder. Over there," he said, pointing to the throne-like chairs of the Luminary Council. "I believe she asked them how they could expect the forgiveness of Faerie when they couldn't even forgive their own. And yes, she is formidable."

So, Meredith was the Fae she'd met yesterday. The one who'd gone for the map.

Tuuli needed to find a way to get a dragon alone. To speak with one about taking her to the cave. She didn't know how to accomplish that.

She didn't know how she'd find the nerve.

CHAPTER 8 ~ ADAIRE

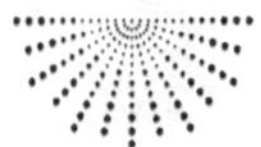

Adaire sat at the table, listening to Tuuli and Dylan talk about dragons.

She sipped her spicy tea, tasting the cinnamon and orange steeped with the tea leaves. Her belly felt full, and she relaxed in the warmth of the room.

Which was unusually crowded. Perhaps it was the snow. She certainly didn't want to go out walking in the forest. Having to make more decisions about which trees she should cut down, and which would survive to thrive again.

Adaire hoped she could be of some help to Tuuli today.

She was acutely aware of Tuuli sitting next to her. The sylph's energy vibrated and touched everything nearby.

And there was something about it that seemed false. Adaire didn't know her at all. And she really knew only one other sylph. Skye.

But Tuuli was being untruthful, or perhaps hiding something.

Adaire trusted her intuition about that.

And she couldn't understand why Tuuli wanted to speak

with a dragon. Air spirits weren't *that* polite. She'd said she was afraid of the dragons. And Tuuli's face blanched white whenever they were mentioned. She really was terrified of them.

Tuuli was a riddle.

An enticing one.

It had been so many millennia since Adaire had taken a lover. Before Faerie had closed the first time. Before Adaire had left her beloved trees, and gone out into the world.

Ashleigh had been a dryad, tall and slender, with pale hair and gray eyes. She'd been the most vital spirit Adaire had ever met. And they'd loved each other and the trees with a passion that Adaire never believed could be replicated.

Ashleigh had been one of those killed by the dragons at the same time as many water Fae. Flamed, along with Ashleigh's beloved forest.

Adaire grieved for millennia. She'd spent too much time drifting and rootless. It had only been recently, when she returned to Faerie, that she began to feel healed from her loss. It didn't hurt so much to see the ash trees, which had grown back in the flamed forest. A monument to Ashleigh.

Adaire had finally let go of her grief and began to retake her life. To heal the forest of Faerie.

And in walked this fluffy sylph who shook everything up. And the sad thing was, she had no idea what even her presence did to Adaire. And perhaps she didn't even care.

The poor air spirit had been tortured and survived. But such things always took a toll. It would be a long time before she recovered.

It would be wrong for Adaire to even mention her feelings, until then.

And dryads and sylphs didn't mix well.

A better match than earth and fire. Or fire and water. But not as easy as earth and earth.

Adaire didn't know how to make all this work out.

What she did know was that Tuuli needed watching. She was like a bomb about ready to go off, and Adaire didn't think anyone could prevent that. And after she did go off, Tuuli would need someone there to pick up the pieces. Adaire meant to make sure that someone would be her.

Which meant following Tuuli around.

She'd have to find a way to do that.

Adaire sipped her lukewarm tea. Watched Tuuli eat. Which she did like a person who was starving. But that was how she seemed to approach everything. With a zest that bordered on craziness.

Dylan and Solange stood to leave the table.

"I've got to go get my sketchbook. I'll come back here and we can wait for Spike to come together."

"All right," said Tuuli. Her face only slightly pale this time.

Adaire watched as Tuuli finished eating the last of her eggs. Then she pushed her plate aside and took a large drink of tea.

Tuuli asked, "Are you going out into the forest today?"

"The Council haven't asked me to return yet. I've got no plans. Except that Aura asked me to keep you company."

"I really do not need company," said Tuuli. "I have always been very self sufficient."

"So you'd like to get rid of me?"

"No. I do not mean that."

"Because I really don't have anything to do. And it's cold to be wandering around in the forest. With the snow, the trees will be sleeping."

"Do trees really sleep?"

"Of course, why wouldn't they?"

"I do not understand trees at all."

"I could teach you," said Adaire.

Tuuli stared at her, a peculiar quirk to her mouth.

"Why would you want to?"

"I love teaching. When I left Faerie and lived with humans, that's what I did. I taught humans how to create healthy and beautiful gardens. I could teach you about the forests of Faerie. If you wanted."

Tuuli was studying her. Adaire had not a clue what she was thinking.

"That might be interesting. I have not spoken to Aura yet. Not really. About what I am to do next. A sylph without wings is no sylph at all. I have no role to serve among the air spirits. I do not know what to do."

"Perhaps you could assist the air spirits who live closer to the ground."

"What do you mean?"

"There are plenty of birds in the forest who stay down near the ground, scavenging on the forest floor. Flies, beetles, butterflies, even the occasional dragonfly. They might need your help."

"I had not considered that. They would still see me as an air spirit. Even without the wings."

"You *are* still an air spirit. There's no mistaking that."

Tuuli opened her mouth, but at that moment Dylan appeared with his pack.

"I'm ready. Spike is coming, I saw him from my window. He'll land anytime."

Tuuli stood. Adaire followed them out of the palace into the freezing cold. The snow still covered everything.

At the same time, there were two large thumps outside and the palace shook.

They were joined by many others from the throne room. Dragons were still a novelty in Faerie.

The second dragon was ruby colored.

Why were there two?

Dylan took Tuuli out to meet Spike.

Adaire took a deep breath and followed them.

The dragons smelled fishy. Their hot breath made clouds of steam in the cold air.

Spike was a black dragon, coal black whose scales were dull, not shiny. From behind his head, all the way down his long neck to the shoulders was covered with spikes. Some looked long and sharp, others shorter and rubbery. He had a short tail, for a dragon. About half the length of his body. Its tip had spikes on all sides. He looked fierce.

The ruby colored dragon was much larger, with shiny scales and had a wavy ridge of flesh above his neck that reminded Adaire of a horse's mane. His tail was twice as long as his body and looked like it could be easily used as a whip.

Dylan introduced Tuuli and Adaire to Spike. He bowed gracefully. Then Dylan introduced them to Keirosum, the ruby colored dragon, who also bowed.

"Ah, you are the one I have come to speak to," the ruby colored dragon said to Tuuli.

"You came to speak to me?" she asked.

"I was told in a vision that you had things to say to me. And a request."

Tuuli's face had turned paler than Adaire had ever seen her.

"I wanted to thank the dragon who saved me from the Fomorian."

"That was Onyx. He knows now. He says you are very welcome. He was honored to rescue you."

Tuuli smiled.

She said, very quietly, but Adaire still overheard, "I would speak with you privately."

"Shall we walk over towards the pools. I feel a great thirst coming upon me."

"That would be lovely."

The ruby dragon and Tuuli moved over by the pools.

Adaire didn't feel she could follow without being rude.

But she watched Tuuli's gestures. The sylph was asked for something. But what?

Dylan had climbed up on top of the riggings of the black dragon.

"See you later," he said.

The dragon soared off over the steps and slowly circled around, gaining height and speed then they flew off over the trees.

Aura came up to Adaire and asked, "How is Tuuli doing?"

"Fine, I think. A little lost."

"I think so too. She feels off. She is putting on a brave front, as humans would say."

Adaire didn't know whether to tell Aura that Tuuli was up to something. She decided not to, until she knew what.

CHAPTER 9 ~ TUULI

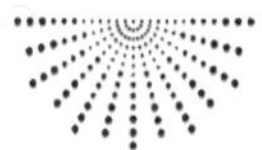

IT WAS THE DARK, COLD OF NIGHT WHEN TUULI crept from her bed. Adaire was sound asleep on the other bed. Dryads obviously slept heavily.

Tuuli felt a bit guilty about leaving without saying anything, but she knew Adaire would try to stop her. She had to do this.

The fire had long since gone out and the room felt cold to her skin. That was okay. Sylphs thrived on the cold. She may have lost her wings, but her blood was true.

Out the window, through the gauzy curtains, the moon was high in the sky, illuminating everything. She could see the branches of trees, white with crystal-like hoar frost. With the nearly full moon, everything was illuminated almost as clearly as day.

Tuuli had gone to bed wearing the heaviest pants and shirt she could find. She tiptoed to the door in her bare feet. The herbal salve had healed her cuts completely. Even her back felt better.

She opened the door slightly, slid through the opening and closed it silently.

Then quickly tiptoed to the stairs and down, barely touching the wood. At the foot of the stairs she found a pair of warm boots, badger fur pants and coat. Leather gloves and a wool hat completed her outfit.

Tuuli didn't know who left them there, but it was exactly what she needed and she dressed quickly.

Trying not to think about the dragon. Or where she was heading.

The smells of baking pasties filled the air. She walked quickly towards the kitchen, stuffing the gloves inside the coat's pockets. Two earth and one fire Fae were there. Baking breakfast pastries and the day's bread.

"Good morning, you are up and about early. Or late," said one of the earth Fae.

"I could not sleep, so I was going out for a walk in the snow, but I smelled the wonderful food you are making in here," said Tuuli.

"Well, we have got several of the pastries done. Take a couple to get you started. There will be more out when you return," said the second earth Fae.

"Thank you," said Tuuli.

She picked up two pastries. The first earth Fae spread a tan cloth napkin on the wooden table and motioned for Tuuli to put the pastries on it.

"You can leave the napkin on one of the tables in the throne room when you return," she said.

Tuuli took a bite of one of the pastries. It was filled with roasted meat and potatoes. And rosemary. It tasted so delicious, she wanted more. But she'd save it for later. She tied them both up in the napkin.

"Thank you so much. This is delicious."

"You are very welcome," said the second earth Fae.

Tuuli left the kitchen and went down the hall to the front door. She put the napkin in one of her pockets, taking the gloves out. The pasties would get smashed, but she would be glad of them before they got to the Fomorian's cave. She'd need all the strength she could get.

Outside, it was bitter cold. And so bright from the snow and moon that she could see Keirosum's hulking form. The palace hadn't needed to light any torches.

As she got closer, Tuuli saw that Keirosum was wearing the same sort of rigging that Dylan's dragon had used.

"Thank you for coming," she said, bowing at him.

"You are very welcome," he said.

She climbed up the rigging and strapped herself into the seat with shaking hands.

He said, "Let us sit for a moment so that our minds may join. Then you will be able to speak to me and give me directions."

This surprised her.

"Did Dylan join minds with his dragon?"

"Spike is too young yet. He does not know how."

"I am also young. Do you think this is something I can do?"

"Can you speak to other Fae with your mind?"

"I have never been taught how to do that. What should I do?"

"Clear your mind of everything but the present. Notice the stillness of the night, the cool temperature, the falling snow. The absence of a breeze. The brilliance of the snow and moon. There are deer in the meadow beyond, I can smell them. I hear little but the sound of our voices."

Tuuli sat, clearing her mind of all but her surroundings. Then she felt a presence. Fiery and hot, strong as a windstorm and just as turbulent.

The fierce voice asked *'Can you hear me?'*

"*Yes,'* she replied.

"*Good. I shall prepare to fly. Hold tight.*"

Tuuli gripped the rigging, hoping it was strong enough.

She felt the dragon's muscles bunch beneath him. He faced the direction of the stairs. Then he began to run, clumsily. It was soon apparent that dragons made poor mounts. She'd never ridden a horse that was this bouncy.

Her light body slammed against the seat again and again with every step, then the dragon reached the top of the steps and he soared over them, his wings flapping thunderously.

How could the entire palace have not heard his arrival? And would they hear his departure?

He flew away from the palace in a circle, gaining a little height. It took three circles before he was above the tree line. Then he headed north.

"*How are you?*" he asked.

Tuuli realized she'd been frozen, holding her breath the entire time.

"*I am fine.*"

"*You are terrified.*"

"*I have always been terrified of dragons. And flying without my wings is not easy.*"

"*You are very brave to do this then. I suppose it would be difficult to fly on another without your own wings for safety. I will take care of you,*" he said.

"*Thank you.*"

They were silent after that.

The feeling of the wind whipping past Tuuli's face made her cry. She hadn't felt it for so long.

Since the last time she'd flown.

She felt it when Keirosum pushed through the boundaries

of Faerie. It felt like dragging a smooth fabric over her body. Then the sensation was gone and they'd left Faerie behind.

The trees melted away and soon they were over farmland. And small towns.

Tuuli's tears dried and her fear of falling faded. As did her fear of the dragon. Perhaps she would fly again with him. When she was not so desperate.

Then she might really enjoy it.

A pang of guilt went through her for leaving Adaire, without telling her where she was going.

She quite liked the dryad. They could be good friends if Adaire ever forgave her for this. She even liked the idea of communing with the lower flying creatures.

But she had to do this first. Had to lead the others to the cave. Had to help rescue the other sylphs.

No matter what the cost.

None of them probably had much time left.

As they flew over the beautiful snow covered countryside, Tuuli tried to plan how they were going to defeat the Fomorian. Or at least immobilize him.

How does one entrap the wind?

CHAPTER 10 ~ ADAIRE

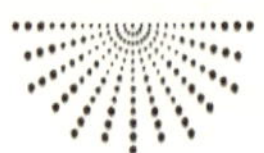

ADAIRE WOKE, STRETCHING AS THE SUN STREAMED into the airy room. She sat up for a minute, trying to remember where she was.

The palace. In Tuuli's room. Filled with white and blue gauzy fabric.

Tuuli's bed was rumpled and empty, but her fresh scent still lingered in the room. She'd probably gone down for breakfast.

Adaire yawned and stood, looking out the window at the serene view. White snow covered everything, making it look pristine and peaceful. The wall near the window felt cold on her naked skin.

Down below, even the opened vault looked clean. Perhaps the snow would do the trick. Be the final cleansing needed to remove the Fomorians' presence from Faerie.

Adaire went down to the first floor, feeling the cold floor beneath her bare feet. Cool air from the front door of the palace wafted past her naked skin. She shivered. Then went to a bathing room to use a shower. The room was tiled in green and white. She set the clothes she'd brought down with her from Tuuli's room, on a tiled bench.

She pretended the shower was a waterfall and the palace transformed the room so that the water seemed to be coming out of stones and she stood in a knee deep pool, edged with boulders and moss.

Afterwards she sat on a flat rock, letting her skin dry and running a wooden comb through her long dark hair.

Her hair was thick and fairly untangled, but there were a few knots that took some work to deal with. Many dryads let their hair tangle into long ropes. When Adaire had gone into the human world, she'd cut her hair. Then she began to brush it, like humans and some of the other Fae. Now it had grown long again and she continued to brush it. She like the silkiness of it.

When she finished, Adaire plaited her waist-length hair into one fat braid. She found some hair supplies on a rock shelf and chose a piece of leather to tie the braid with.

After drying, she slid into a pair of mossy green pants and a loose shirt. And a pair of tan, soft leather boots.

Then she went to the throne room, where the aroma of meat filled pastries caught her nose, making her stomach rumble.

She looked for Tuuli, but didn't see her. Adaire sat down at a table with Solange and Dylan. She loaded a plate with several pastries and poured a mug of tea. Today's blend was malty, but sharp tasting. Black tea with an extra kick. She added some fresh cream to take the edge off it.

The pastry was as delicious as it smelled. Crispy and flaky and soft all at the same time. The filling was roasted beef with potatoes, rosemary and a luscious gravy. It was extremely satisfying. She only had one before moving on to a sweet berry filled one.

Aura came and sat next to her.

"How is Tuuli doing?" she asked.

"I haven't seen her this morning, but she was fine last night. A little wired, I think."

"Wired?" asked Aura.

"It's a human expression. Tightly strung. Keyed up. Anxious."

"About what?"

"She wouldn't say. I don't know. There was something going on between her and the ruby colored dragon. They were very private. But I can't imagine what it would be. Tuuli's terrified of the dragons."

"Wait, you said you did not see her this morning?" asked Aura.

"She was gone when I woke up. I showered and came here."

"She has not been in here. I was the first one here this morning. And I have been here the entire time."

"Where could she be?" asked Adaire.

"I do not know," said Aura. Her gaze looked far off.

"After I finish eating, I'll go look for her."

"Thank you. She is so young."

Aura moved off to talk to Fae at another table.

Adaire turned to look at Dylan and Solange.

"She couldn't have gone far," said Solange. "It's very cold out."

"She's a sylph. When they're healthy they thrive on the cold."

"Is she healthy?" asked Solange.

"She's recovering very quickly. And she's young. So yes."

Solange looked thoughtful and asked, "How old is she?"

"Probably only a thousand years or so," said Adaire.

Solange shook her head and said, "Wow."

"I know, it's a long time, if you're a human."

"I don't think I'll ever fit in here."

"You already do," said Adaire, touching Solange's hand.

"Thank you."

Dylan put his arm around Solange.

"Told you," he said.

"I know. It's just that sometimes I feel like I have nothing in common with any of you."

Adaire said, "You have more in common with Fae, than there are differences."

After breakfast Adaire searched the palace, but didn't find Tuuli. She bundled up in a coat and heavy boots, gloves and hat to go outside. As she was leaving the palace, she met Dylan coming in.

"You'd better hear this," he said.

She followed him outside where Spike stood, waiting for him.

"Tell her what you told me," said Dylan.

"Dylan told me that the air spirit who was here yesterday is missing. Keirosum met her during the night and they flew off towards the North. Following the others."

"Why?" asked Adaire.

"She knows the way to the cave where the other sylphs are imprisoned," said Spike.

"Is she safe?"

Spike was silent for a minute, as if listening.

"For the present. They are at the far range of my ability to hear Keirosum."

"Could you follow them?" asked Adaire.

"I could, but this rigging can only carry one. Shall I call another dragon?"

"Yes," Dylan. "Call two."

"You can't go," said Adaire.

"Not me. We'll find a couple of fire or stone Fae to go."

"I'm going," said Adaire.

"Why?"

"I have to."

"You're scared stiff of dragons."

"I have to go."

"It's not your fault Tuuli slipped away."

"No, it's not, but I'm still going," said Adaire, her hands on her hips.

"Okay, call three dragons," said Dylan. "Let's go round up a couple others to go along."

Adaire followed him into the palace.

Why was she doing this? Hadn't she had enough of Fomorians?

She needed to go help Tuuli. Otherwise she'd just worry. And she didn't want to be away from her. As long as there was a possibility of love. And since Tuuli didn't know, the possibility was there.

Dylan said, "I'll go get escorts. You go to the kitchen and get food for three, no four. Tuuli probably didn't bring much."

"What about water?" asked Adaire.

"Bring a little, but there will probably be snow to melt."

Adaire went to the kitchen.

The palace Fae quickly packed a basket woven from reeds, with food. They put into it two metal bottles filled with water and stopped with plugs.

The basket closed and could be tied onto the dragon's rigging.

Adaire took it and went back out to the front of the palace. Aura was there, holding a pair of deerskin pants and a fur coat made from seal.

"I should have known she would try to go back," said Aura, while Adaire added the extra layer of clothes.

"None of us knew."

"I knew. She has always been impulsive. And more courageous than most of us. She will be a very powerful Fae when she is older."

"Provided she lives that long," said Dylan, who came out of the throne room with Pearce, a stone warrior.

Pearce, Dylan and Adaire had escaped from the Fomorians together and had a close bond. She hugged him.

"Egan is coming too," said Dylan. "He's getting his things."

Egan had been in the same cell as her when the Fomorians captured them. She felt relieved at both of the Fae's help.

"I've never ridden a dragon before," said Pearce. "This should be interesting."

Adaire tried not to think about it.

CHAPTER 11 ~ TUULI

THEY WERE FLYING OVER MORE FROZEN LAND. IT HAD gotten much colder and the air felt bumpier.

Tuuli rarely had flown this high. After the first part of the night, she'd put her gloved hands in the warm coat pockets, grateful she was strapped into the rigging. Although, the dragon's flight was smooth.

He seemed tireless.

He merely followed where she pointed to with her mind.

Her stomach rumbled, but Tuuli knew she needed to save the food. She could wait. Still, she was thirsty. She thought of the taste of fresh strawberries, making the flavor of them real, trying to get her mouth to water and make some moisture for her parched throat.

They were flying over a river of moving metal. Humans, in their machines, moved quickly down the gray river. Another Fae had once told her that the river was hard, like stone.

"How is it that you remain unseen by humans?"

"They would not believe it if they did see me. But I make myself invisible to them. Transparent. They see only the sky surrounding me."

"Will we fly all day?"

"No. From the picture you have shown me in your mind, we will stop at the halfway point. I must rest. When I land we will sleep. But that will not be for a while yet."

"Do you know where the others are?"

"I cannot find them yet. They are still too far away."

Tuuli watched the land beneath her flow by. The sun peered up from beneath them, promising a bright blue day. It would continue to be cold though.

Her body ached from being in one position for hours. And her back wounds still hurt.

She could hear nothing but the whoosh of wind past her ears, muffled by the hat. At least the voice on the wind was from the dragon's speed and not a Fomorian.

Tuuli shifted on the seat, stretching her back and legs.

Her mind had yet to come up with a plan that might work to defeat or distract the Fomorian.

Other than her sacrifice.

Tuuli didn't know if she was willing to do that. Or brave enough to. But if she did, perhaps she could divert the Fomorian long enough for the others to be freed. And escape.

She dreaded the confrontation.

But it had to be done.

Tuuli hoped the stone and fire warriors would have come up with a better plan by the time she caught up with them. And she would catch up. She knew exactly where the cave was. They merely had a rough idea.

It seemed only a bit later that they crossed the sea. Not the first sea she had swam. But the second.

Fae had no names for these lands. Or if they had, the names were long lost. Since Faerie had closed, most Fae had stayed within Faerie's boundaries. At least those who had not forsaken Faerie. Like Meredith. And Egan, Dylan, Skye, and Adaire.

Tuuli had always thought of those who left as traitors. That's what she'd been taught.

But they had returned. At least those still alive.

And Egan had ruled Faerie. And now Meredith was on the Council of Luminaries.

So had she been wrong?

They must not be traitors if Faerie accepted them back. And gave them power. The essence of Faerie would not have done such a thing if they were corrupt Fae. She would not have put them into places where they could control the fate of Faerie.

Unless Faerie was herself injured or deluded.

Was that even possible?

Hours later, as the sun had crested the horizon, Keirosum headed towards a snow-covered, hilly area near the north coast of the land. Tuuli recognized it as where she swam across the narrow sea, after her escape from the cave. She'd gotten out of the water here and began walking.

There was a small town nearby, but Keirosum landed on a hill that looked like it was snow covered grass.

Tuuli's legs felt numb from being in one position so long. She stood and climbed down the rigging, falling when she tried to stand.

"Are you all right?"

"I will be. Just need to stretch out my legs."

"We will rest here. I am too tired to fly longer. It will be a long night. You might want to sleep. Crawl under my wing and I will keep you warm."

"Okay. Can you hear the others?"

"They await us. They have not found the cave yet."

Tuuli stumbled around the field for a time until her legs

worked again. The field was on a cliff overlooking the sea. The wind whipped past her so strongly it was difficult to stand.

She stopped and ate another bite of the pastry. She really should share.

"I have some food, not much, but if you would like this, it is yours," she said, holding up the second pastry.

"I will take half, if you would divide it for me," he said.

She broke it in half and put part on the ground in front of him.

He licked it up delicately with his long tongue and closed his mouth, chewing.

"Now that was lovely. I have only heard of Faerie food, never actually eaten it. Quite a delicacy. Thank you. That will give me more strength than you could have imagined."

"You are welcome," she said.

What did he mean it would give him more strength than she imagined?

Faerie food was known for being concentrated and powerful. Magical even. Did it have a stronger affect on dragons?

There was so much about the outside world she didn't know. Dragons were from the outside world, and had been her entire life.

She could smell the salt of the sea from here. The last time she'd smelled it, her lungs had been too full of salty water. From a wave she hadn't noticed.

This time at least she was dry. Hopefully, she'd stay that way.

The wind here was vicious and bitterly cold. But it felt natural. No Fomorians present that she could sense. And she'd gotten better at sensing them.

She continued to chew her bite of the pastry. The meat and

sauce tasted rich and felt satisfying. The potato promised to keep her feeling full for a while at least. Once again, she thanked the kitchen Fae. She hoped to get a chance to do it again in person.

Finally, the wind was too cold. She took shelter beneath one of Keirosum's giant wings and fell asleep next to the heat of his body. Amazing how much heat a dragon put out. Even in this frigid place.

Tuuli fell asleep, dreaming. Remembering as a child how she used to hold a orange and black butterfly on the palm of her hand. Its wings had bluish-white eyes on them. The butterfly flew and then landed on her again. Flew away and returned. When it sat on her hand, she promised it long life. It had come to see her every day for a time and she'd had long conversations with it.

Perhaps Adaire had the right idea.

CHAPTER 12 ~ ADAIRE

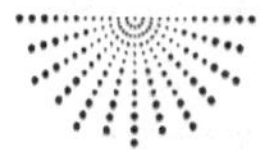

ADAIRE STOOD OUTSIDE THE PALACE AT ABOUT midday in the blinding snow and sun, staring at the three dragons. A large opal colored male, named Ethelgarde. A topaz colored male, named Iru. And an emerald colored female, called Goshania.

All three were known to Faerie, they had been the first dragons to appear, as ambassadors.

They smelled slightly fishy. Adaire supposed they probably dove headlong into a school of fish and just opened their mouths, swallowing several as a meal.

She took a deep breath and walked up to the opal colored one.

"I'm Adaire," she said, bowing formally. "Will you carry me. We are in need of great speed."

"I am Ethelgarde, I would be honored to carry you."

"I have never ridden a dragon before. I'm very afraid."

"I will take care of you. This rigging has been checked and it is very strong. I will do everything in my power to keep you safe from harm."

"Thank you," she said. That was probably about the most assurance she was going to get from a dragon. From anyone.

Adaire climbed up the rigging with the basket of food, feeling particularly clumsy in her heavy clothing. But she was sure she'd be glad of it after hours in the cold wind.

She took off the gloves to strap the basket and herself in tightly. The harness and seat allowed her to shift a little.

"I'm ready," she said.

She noticed Pearce and Egan were strapped in as well.

Pearce rode the emerald dragon and Egan the topaz.

Ethelgarde moved to take off first.

He walked to the end of the plaza, by the fountains and turned around. Which was an amazing feat due to his great bulk.

"I am going to run off the edge and begin flying," he said, to her mind.

Which surprised her. She didn't know dragons could send. That would make communication much easier.

"I'm ready," she sent.

He shot forward, picking up speed and then his great wings went out and he soared as the ground dropped away.

A crowd had gathered off to the side, standing on the stairs. They applauded as he took off. Adaire couldn't hear, she just saw them clapping. The only thing she could hear was his wings.

He circled, gaining speed and altitude, and his wings thundered.

The sound was muffled only slightly by her hat.

As they circled higher she watched as Goshania, and Iru in turn, took off. When they all were flying high enough, the three of them turned, Ethelgarde in the lead, and flew off to the North.

It took some time before Adaire could relax her grip on the rigging.

The view was breathtaking. She'd flown in an airplane once. It had been terrifying. This was actually a little better. She trusted living creatures more than machines built and maintained by humans.

"Does Keirosum know we are coming?" she asked him.

"He is too far away to hear us. Do you want him to know or shall we conceal ourselves?"

"Tell him to stop when he can first hear you. We need to catch up."

"I will do that then. It is possible that he will get to his destination before he will be able to hear us."

"Well, there is nothing else we can do, is there?"

"No."

They passed through the boundary of Faerie and Adaire felt a tug on her, the mournfulness of leaving home.

Down below, in a meadow stood three Fomorians. She recognized Ùisdean the earthquake, Cethlenn the fog, and the Blizzard. So the original Fomorians had joined with their offspring. The Council probably already knew that.

The earthquake was shaking down a grove of ash trees. Even though they were outside of Faerie, she still grieved for them.

She felt grateful for the warm furs. The cold wind blasted past her. After a time her body began to ache and she shifted position slightly.

She hoped that at least this trek would help vanquish her fear of dragons. It seemed that they were to regain their place in Faerie.

Adaire only wished that they'd been able to help rid Faerie of the Fomorians.

After what seemed like a very long time they passed out of

Ireland and over the sea to Scotland. Of course Faerie didn't use those names. Humans did. But Adaire had spent a couple thousand years among humans. Long enough to learn their world's geography.

The air over the sea was colder and bumpier. Adaire tightened her grip on the rigging. The sun was setting on the horizon.

Flying over the sea at night. Not how she wanted to die.

Hours later, the darkness seemed interminable. Finally, she began to see distant lights. Boats? Then a glow in front of them. As they grew closer to the glow, she realized it was a town.

Ethelgarde shifted course, flying North of the town, avoiding its bright lights.

Sometime during the night flight, Iru had taken the lead and Ethelgarde fell back to take advantage of the air current moved by Iru's wings. What was it called when geese flew in an inverted V behind the others? She couldn't remember.

The flight continued for several more hours. Most of the time over uninhabited land. Or perhaps people had simply turned all their lights out and gone to bed. At any rate there were few lights to be seen. She couldn't actually see the land. It was too dark and they were too high.

"We are going to land soon, to rest," said Ethelgarde.

"Okay."

Adaire hung on. Even with the warning she was started when the dark land rose up quickly beneath them. The dragon had turned his wings sideways to slow down. He landed running and slowed to a walk.

She could hear the crash of waves against rock and smelled salty kelp. Once Ethelgarde stopped, Adaire unbuckled the harness and climbed down. Her legs, stuck on one position for so long, had turned squishy and non-functional.

The other dragons had landed first. Pearce and Egan were waiting for her.

"We need to tell the Council that the Fomorians have joined forces with their offspring," she said.

"It's already done," said Pearce. "Goshania told Attania, and she flew to Faerie to tell the Council."

"Have they been in contact with Keirosum yet?" she asked.

"No. They're still to far away."

"Where are we going?" asked Adaire.

"Iceland, probably."

She sighed.

"Did you bring food?" asked Egan.

"Oh, I'll get it, it's still on the rigging."

She climbed back up and unstrapped the basket of food and brought it to the others. They stood, tired of sitting and ate cold meaty pastries and drank a bit of water.

She offered a pastry to each of the dragons and they ate them, grateful for the gesture. It probably didn't go very far. The dragons were so huge.

They bowed at her and Ethelgarde said, "That is indeed a treat. We have only heard tales of the food of Faerie."

After everyone had finished eating, drinking and stretching, Adaire fastened the basket back on the rigging. It wouldn't do to forget it.

Ethelgarde said, "You would do well to sleep now. Come beneath my wing and I will keep you warm. Otherwise, you will freeze."

She felt exhausted. How could one be exhausted just from sitting all day?

Before long she was curled up warm and asleep.

What would daylight bring?

Even if they found Tuuli, would they be of any help. Or would Tuuli simply resent her?

CHAPTER 13 ~ TUULI

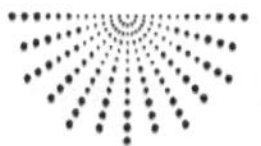

Tuuli pointed Keirosum towards the slope where she'd crawled out of the cave. It was probably an old gas vent for the ancient volcano. One that she hoped was still sleeping.

The large cave opening was on the other side of the mountain. That's where she'd been brought in when first captured, but the Fomorian blocked that one. Blowing his wind out through the wide entrance, unless others were bringing in captives.

Keirosum landed softly on the rocky ground. Tuuli climbed down the rigging and stood in the blasting wind off the sea. The slope was slippery and icy. There was a range of large boulders down to small, sharp stones to gritty sand. It was difficult to walk on with boots, but there was no way she'd take them off. Her cuts hadn't been healed that long.

"The others are on their way here. They will be invisible to us and everyone. Just as we are."

"You can do that?"

"We dragons can do many things," he said, coughing that hoarse cough which she'd come to realize was a laugh.

"You should eat the rest of your food. You will need the strength," he said.

"But if we rescue the others, they will surely need food."

"If you are not strong enough, there will be no rescue. Only sacrifice. I would not have that."

Tuuli dug the mashed pastry out of her pocket. She ate half of it and gave the other half to the dragon.

"You will need your strength, too."

"Thank you."

Waiting seemed interminable.

It was dark, the middle of the night. But sylphs could see well enough in the dark. As could dragons, Keirosum had told her. Flying creatures needed to be able to find a safe place to land in the dark.

The dragon curled up to sleep, while he waited.

Tuuli grew tired of the wind blasting around the peak and sought shelter beneath his warm wing. His hide was scaly, but each scale was polished to a smoothness that made Faerie glass look primitive.

He really was quite a beautiful creature. His scales, which looked ruby at first, also held an orange red color. In the right light, his scales shimmered between the two shades.

Tuuli had only seen two dragons up close, Spike and Keirosum. They were both so different. Spike was a dull, black color with spiky protrusions around his neck. Did shininess come from age?

Keirosum had a flaring ridge along the back of his neck. He looked elegant with his extra long tail. Tuuli had a hunch it could be used as a formidable weapon.

She must have dozed off, because the next thing she knew

there was thundering in the air. It sounded like Keirosum's wings magnified a dozen times.

She tried to go out and look, but he blocked her way.

"Wait or you will be blown off the mountain."

Then eventually, the noise stopped.

She crawled out from beneath his wings, but saw nothing.

"Who is there?" she sent.

"I am Aidan. A fire Fae. And you?"

"Tuuli. A sylph."

"Is this the place?"

"We are close. How many of there are you?"

"There are twenty four of us. Not all of us have room to land at this spot. The others have landed nearby."

Tuuli could see the sun peeking over the horizon, beginning to light up the landscape. It was all rocks, snow and ice. As the sun rose higher, she could see clear outlines of the dragons. It was as if they were transparent.

She and the other Fae had gathered together, all of them invisible. Although there was some question as to whether the Fomorians could see them. Humans couldn't, but Fomorians had magic. They were speaking, discussing a plan.

Keirosum said to her mind, *"Return quickly. More Fomorians are coming. They must not see your glow."*

She ran to hide beneath his wing, the other Fae hid beneath their dragons.

"How many are there?" she asked.

"Two. Both of them winds. They are alone. They carry no prisoners. They are small winds. Weak. Not as strong as one of the winds we fought near Faerie."

She finally sat down on the damp earth where Keirosum's body had melted the ice. Waiting. Then eventually, she lay down. To sleep. She'd need to be awake later.

It was evening, when Keirosum woke her at last.

"Two of the winds have departed," he said, speaking out loud, although very quietly. "A massive one, we think it must be Conand, the North Wind. And a smaller one, one of the winds who came this morning."

"So, we don't know how many are in the cave."

"We can but hope there is only one of the small winds. The wind whipping around the peaks has died down."

Tuuli met with the other Fae again. They argued back and forth, before finally deciding on a plan.

She would lead them down the vent, since she knew the way. Several of the dragons would stay on the ground and guard the vent. The others would attack the large cave opening, diverting the wind's attention from the prisoners.

As Tuuli waited in the darkness for the other Fae whose dragons had landed farther down the mountain to arrive, she stared upwards.

The sky began to light up. She'd rarely seen the glowing colors.

The Fae called them the shining ones. Green, blue, and purple lights streamed across the sky, slowly moving. It was as if the gods were dancing above her.

The stone and fire Fae joined her, entranced by the movement of the light. The magic was worth the hardships of the journey.

She hoped to live through the night and see them again.

"Call me if you need help," said Keirosum.

"I will. Thank you. Although if I'm deep in the tunnel or inside the cave you might not be able to do much."

"I will break the cave entrance apart to help you."

"Thank you." Tuuli tied the heavy coat and hat in a bundle, onto the dragon's rigging. Just in case they had to take off

quickly. They were too bulky and hot for climbing down the vent.

When everyone was gathered, Tuuli took a deep breath and slipped down the hole.

The rock inside was slick and icy. She remembered that from climbing out. She had nearly frozen trying to get out. Aidan followed close behind her. All of the Fae were going in. It would take that many to open the cages. And some Fae would need to be carried out.

The vent was a long one. She went slowly down into the cramped tunnel. Being able to touch all sides of it was helpful. She could brace herself on the steep places, so she didn't slide down, out of control.

Then she came to the spot where two vents converged in the large one which led down. The vent on the right was the one she'd taken from the surface, she didn't know where the other one went. She sent to the last Fae coming down to stay there and direct people going up to take the right vent.

The rock here was smooth and slippery. Tuuli felt grateful for the leather palmed gloves which gripped well.

She could smell the stench of the Fomorian now. Amazing that a wind could smell so foul.

Did that mean there were more here?

Tuuli remembered it always smelled that badly. And when she escaped, there had only been one wind guarding the cave. But then the imprisoned Fae probably didn't smell that great either.

Tuuli kept crawling downwards into the depths of the mountain. It grew slightly warmer and the scent made her nauseous.

Was the warmth coming from the volcano? Maybe it wasn't totally asleep. Maybe it was preparing to wake up. She hadn't remembered it being this warm, but then she'd been starving, wounded and weak.

As she moved down the tunnel it grew slightly lighter.

They were getting close.

The smell grew awful.

Filth, blood, sweat and death.

She wasn't looking forward to seeing what they would find.

She stopped and sent to the others, *"We are almost there. Be ready to move quickly."*

The vent curved a bit. Just around the curve was the small opening.

She climbed out and as quietly as possible, down a pile of rubble. There was a partial rock wall in front of her. After she gotten out of her cage, she'd run back here to hide until she could find a way out. Discovering the vent upwards had been sheer luck.

The others gathered around her.

She sent, *"On the other side of this wall are the cages. There are many."*

Aidan nodded and she could see the distant look in his eyes. He was sending the message to the dragons to attack the cave opening.

Tuuli's entire body tensed, her muscles tight. It had been that way since she entered the vent. Some of the tension had dissipated by moving. Waiting here, hidden, just made it worse.

She tried to take deep breaths, to calm herself like she'd learned as a child. It wasn't working.

There was a roaring on the other side of the stone wall. It sounded like a huge windstorm. And there was the thunder of dragons' wings. And bellowing. She'd never heard that before. Was it pain or something else?

Aidan sent, *"Go!"*

Everyone winked into invisibility, and she felt them leave the safety of their hiding spot.

They were working in teams. The fire Fae would soften the metal locks on the cages and the stone warriors would hammer them until they broke.

Tuuli cast a glamour of invisibility over herself and went out to the main part of the cavern.

She strengthened herself for the cold metal and went inside the first cage pulling a weak sylph of of it. She half carried the young sylph, whose name she'd forgotten.

"Wake up," she whispered. "Time to escape."

The Fae whimpered.

"Quiet now."

At least the young one still had her wings.

She took her back to the vent and said, "Climb up the shaft. There are dragons outside, waiting to help."

The sylph looked alarmed.

"It is all right. They are our friends. Now go. Follow the vent to the right. I must help the others."

The sylph climbed over the rubble and up the tube.

Tuuli went back for another.

She made more trips than she could count. All the sylphs were so very weak. Some would have to be carried up the vent. Those she left in the rubble as she went back for more.

She could see the shadowy figures of dragons hovering, darting in and firing flames at the Fomorian.

He stood in the mouth of the cave. Looking like a whirlpool of wind, the roaring of his power was like being in a massive windstorm.

And this was the weak one. Tuuli shivered.

His wind was being forced out of the cave at least.

As she pulled another sylph from a cage, the Fomorian turned slightly to the left and caught part of the mouth of the cave in his wind. Then hurled the chunks of stone at the dragons.

Most of them dodged out of the way. But a blue one was hit full in the chest and thrown backwards screaming.

It was awful to hear.

Tuuli tried to work faster.

By now, most of the cages were open.

They sylphs who could walk and were strong enough, helped those who couldn't move, up the vent. Dragging or carrying them.

Tuuli was out of breath. Panting.

Aidan said, "Go up the vent. Help them. We've got enough Fae down here to get everyone else out."

"No, I'm okay."

"That's not it. They need help. None of them have seen dragons. My dragon says they're panicking."

"Oh."

"Now go."

Tuuli took the hand of one of the sylphs who'd been badly beaten. She wasn't very steady on her feet, but could move.

"Come, let me help you," she said.

The sylph nodded, unable to speak. She probably needed water. Once up top, there would be snow to eat.

Tuuli pulled her up the vent tube.

Finally, the sylph could move by herself, half crawling up. It didn't matter. No one in front of them was moving very quickly. Everyone was in such bad shape.

She sent a message to them, *"Hurry please. We must get out of the tube. There are more coming up behind. We have to get everyone out. And back to Faerie."*

Tuuli had no idea how they were going to give any of the sylphs enough food to get them back.

After her escape, she'd picked dried berries, but that hadn't been till she'd swum across the sea. Twice. She hadn't found berries until she'd gotten to the mainland. And even then, it wasn't much.

And then she'd had to walk for days and days and days. And swim again.

Were there enough dragons to take everyone?

She hoped so.

The Fae in front of her were moving a bit faster now.

It still seemed to take forever to get through the tunnel. Her muscles ached. She was thankful for the gloves though. Her hands would have been cut and bleeding.

Like the first time.

Like all the other captive Faes' limbs were.

Finally, she could smell the fresh cold air.

Up at the mouth of the tunnel, she sensed things clogging up.

"Keep moving up. We've got to get out. The dragons are here to help us. They are part of your rescue."

That got things moving.

When she was almost to the top and could see dim daylight, the entire mountain rumbled and shook.

The volcano?

She tried sending her senses out while climbing.

Tuuli could only sense air. Moving quickly.

The Fomorian.

He had turned his attention inward. Towards the cave.

"Dragons! Attack the cave mouth!" Tuuli sent.

The air turned hot.

The Fae in front of her sensed the urgency and began to move faster.

There were Fae at the top, strong enough to pull the others out.

Someone grabbed her arms and hauled her out of the hole and to the side. Then those Fae turned back for another.

It was terribly bright. The cave had been so dark.

Tuuli moved away from the hole. It looked like hundreds of Fae in various states of mobility. Some had climbed onto the dragons and were being strapped onto the rigging. One dragon was taking off, loaded down with almost twenty Fae.

She hoped the rigging was strong enough.

Others were lying on the ice, shoveling it into their mouths.

Several sylphs were flying off after the dragon. Some of the flying Fae were carrying others.

As soon as the dragon took off, another landed and injured Fae were helped up by those who could lift them.

An arm grabbed her.

"Tuuli. Get on a dragon," said Aidan.

"Is everyone out?"

"Yes, almost. The last are just coming out. But the Fomorian is in the vent we think. We'll be under attack soon. Get on a dragon. Now."

Tuuli ran for one of the dragons, but it was full. She went to another one, but it too was full.

Finally, she saw Keirosum landing. She ran to him, scrambling up the rigging.

"Nice to see you little one."

"I'm grateful to see you too." She felt so relieved.

Tuuli helped other Fae tie themselves onto the rigging. They all looked terrified.

There was a black dragon being loaded and then everyone would be aboard a dragon.

Keirosum said, loudly, "I'm going to take off. Everyone hang on tightly."

He ran off the edge of the slope and soared over the sea.

Tuuli turned to see behind. The black dragon flew off the mountain and turned, diving back towards the vent. It shot a massive flame towards the opening and pivoted with a snap of its wings, it dropped and flew away from the mountain just as a loud explosion happened. The vent they'd crawled through just moments before erupted in flame.

Keirosum flew faster.

The black dragon wasn't carrying as many Fae and caught up.

Then Tuuli saw five other dragons coming around the side of the mountain. They were carrying no one and sped quickly away from the explosion.

"*What happened?*" she sent to Keirosum.

"*They've trapped the Fomorian in the cave. They closed the large opening. The Fomorian tried to escape through the vent. Carbon just sealed it. But I'm afraid the Fomorian woke up the volcano. The mountain is alive again.*"

Tuuli looked back at the exploding mountain. Was it a Fomorian too? Some volcanoes were.

That would mean the wind Fomorian wouldn't be trapped anymore. Was he still alive? Could a wind Fomorian survive an exploding volcano?

She didn't want to think about it.

She was absolutely exhausted.

It was all she could do to hang on to the rigging.

She hoped all the others could do the same.

CHAPTER 14 ~ ADAIRE

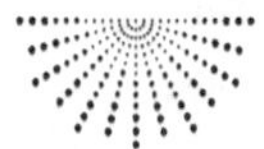

ADAIRE SAT ATOP ETHELGARDE. THEY HAD PASSED over Scotland and were flying towards Iceland she guessed. Then suddenly, he turned and flew East.

"Where are we going?"

"We have found Keirosum and the others. They are on an island. There are too many Fae for them to carry any farther. We will lighten their load, so we can all fly faster."

"Is Tuuli among them?"

He was silent for a while, as if listening.

Finally, he said, *"Tuuli is safe among them. But the volcano is erupting. And the Fomorian may or may not be dead. He is a wind. If he is alive, he will be looking for us."*

Ethelgarde picked up speed, as did Goshania and Iru. She couldn't see them, they were invisible as was Ethelgarde, but she could hear the thundering of their wings.

The sun was setting in glorious colors.

Adaire looked towards where she thought Iceland would be, but could see only clouds. Were they clouds of steam or ash?

It seemed to take forever to get to the island. She couldn't see any dragons anywhere. But thundering increased as they neared several white mounds rising out of the sea.

As darkness grew, she could barely see the islands as they closed in. An aurora, the shining ones, danced in the sky. Waves of green, purple and red lights moved across the sky, sometimes hidden by the clouds, other times revealed in all their glory.

As they neared the islands, Ethelgarde, Goshania and Iru shimmered into visibility. The dragons on the ground did the same.

Adaire gasped. She counted twenty five dragons down there. Between the dragons, small figures ran around like ants. As they flew closer, she saw Fae.

Ethelgarde and the others landed. Adaire climbed down the rigging. There were so many dragons, she couldn't see Keirosum. She remembered he was ruby colored, but there were several red dragons.

"*Tuuli,*" she sent. There was no response.

"Don't go far," said Ethelgarde. "We will have to load up quickly and fly off in a hurry. The debris from the volcano is blowing this way."

"I just want to find Tuuli. I can't sense her. She isn't responding."

"I think you would be better off helping the injured Fae get tied onto the rigging," he said, a note of sadness in his voice.

"You're right. Of course."

Several of them were coming her way. Some of the stronger ones were carrying the weaker.

Adaire went to them and lifted one of the unconscious Fae from the arms of another.

She lifted the sylph easily. How could a living being weigh so little?

Ethelgarde was one of the larger dragons. He took twenty Fae plus Adaire.

Once the Fae had been as evenly distributed as possible, the dragons began to take off. In groups of five. They flew for the rest of the night and all the next day.

As they flew Adaire put her hands on the arms of the unconscious Fae closest to her. She sent healing energy through her fingers into the sylph. Trying to help her recover a little more quickly. The sylph opened her eyes and a look of panic crossed her face.

"Rest. You are safe. We are on our way to Faerie."

The panic turned to astonishment and the sylph sat quietly for a time and then fell asleep.

Adaire hoped Faeries' healers were ready for the influx of injured Fae.

She was grateful for the warm furs as they flew night and day.

Adaire opened the basket and passed all the pastries out. Fae would take a bite and pass them on until everyone had some. She did the same with the water bottles.

How could the dragons last so long? Surely they must be exhausted.

It was night again. Adaire had lost track of everything. She was thirsty and hungry. She hadn't taken any food or water. The others needed it more.

They had flown over cities and roads filled with white and red tail lights. Dark places that must be farmland or wilderness.

Then she saw it. Glowing. The boundary of Faerie was

glowing. It was as if someone had turned on an entire street of Christmas lights in the darkness. Adaire hadn't known Faerie could do that.

She nudged the Fae around her and could see their faces light up in the darkness.

The dragons streamed through the boundary.

Adaire could feel the land welcoming them.

Home. They were home. Safe.

"We are coming," she sent to the palace. *"We need healers. And food and drink for the injured Fae. And food and drink for the dragons."*

As the dragons flew lower, just over the tree tops the air warmed.

They circled the palace, waiting for the weakest dragons to land first. Ethelgarde was one of the last to land.

She didn't see how he was going to find the space, but he slowed down so much with his wings, that he dropped onto the road below the palace and only had to walk five steps before stopping. His nose was right up against a building. He backed up slowly and stopped, lying down with a groan.

Adaire climbed down the rigging first, her legs felt rubbery. At the bottom, she helped the other Fae down until everyone was off. She pointed them towards the palace up the stairs.

"There should be food and drink and healers up there," she said.

Then she went to Ethelgarde's head and asked, "Are you all right?"

"I am so tired, I just want to sleep for days."

Two stone Fae came down the stairs, lugging a huge container of water.

Ethelgarde raised his head.

"Is that for me?"

"Of course," said one.

Ethelgarde began drinking.

Another Fae came carrying a platter of pastries. They smelled delicious. But Adaire didn't take one. She had the Fae set it down within Ethelgarde's reach.

He finished drinking and then sniffed.

The dragon looked at the pastries and then Adaire. She gestured with her arms that they were for him. He stuck out his tongue and delicately began to eat them all, one by one. In the end, he picked several of them up with his front feet and his claws.

Adaire put her hand on his neck and said, "Thank you, my friend. When you've finished eating, please, just sleep. You are welcome here."

He looked at her strangely.

"Have I said something wrong?"

"No. It is just that no Fae has ever called me friend."

"I would like to be your friend."

"You are no longer afraid of me?"

"No. I am not."

"Good," he said. "Now, I will sleep. You should go eat and sleep. I can see you are tired. And you must be hungry."

"I am," she said. "I will see you tomorrow. Or perhaps the day after. When you wake again."

"If you can't find me, just call. I will be able to hear."

She smiled at him and climbed up the steps to the palace. Wherever there was a landing, a dragon lay. Eating or sleeping.

Adaire felt sure that from the air it would look as if dragons were strewn everywhere.

It was difficult to climb all the way up to the top of the stairs, her legs felt so tired. But she finally made it.

There were throngs of Fae everywhere. It seemed as if all of Faerie had come out to greet the sylphs.

As they should.

A kitchen Fae was walking through the crowd with a tray of steaming mugs. Adaire took one and it turned out to be hot mead. She sipped the honey wine and it warmed her in return. She had grown chilled from exhaustion.

It was time to rest. She finished the mead and set the mug down on a short wall surrounding the courtyard.

Another Fae came past with a tray of pastries.

Adaire took a pastry and bit into it. Raspberries and a creamy cheese. It tasted like summer. She ate the entire thing so quickly, it was as if it had never been.

Still, she felt satisfied.

She considered joining what must have been a mass of Fae in the throne room. She saw Tuuli helping another sylph into the palace. Her arms around the slender young woman, whose wings drooped. Tuuli looked tired, but her face was radiant.

Adaire felt like she'd been punching in the stomach.

Tuuli was in her element. With her people. She didn't need Adaire any more.

Adaire felt too tired and too lost to be around others.

She walked back down the steps. For a moment she considered sleeping in the warmth of Ethelgarde's wing, but she missed her trees. And solitude called to her. The forest had healed her once before.

Adaire crossed the stone road and the grassy meadow. She passed through groves of several types of trees until coming to her beloved oaks. The forest was sleeping, listening to the celebration, but sleeping. It was quiet here. She found a lovely mossy hollow in the trunk of an ancient oak tree.

And curled up in it, feeling the softness of the moss against her bare cheek. She still wore the fur coat and pants. And the warm hat, gloves and boots. Adaire was too tired to take them off, even though she was warm now from the inside.

She fell asleep, weeping, even though the images of the shining ones danced on the inside of her eyelids.

CHAPTER 15 ~ TUULI

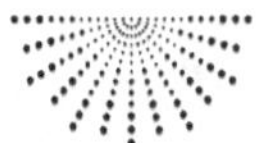

TUULI STOOD IN THE THRONE ROOM. SHE STILL WORE her fur coat and pants, the heavy boots and warm hat. She'd taken the gloves off, putting them in her pockets, to help the others. The room was roasting hot, but she still felt cold.

She'd been too busy bringing injured Fae inside to think to undress. But now it looked like everyone was taken care of.

The room bustled with healers of all elements although Aura was the only air healer working. Kitchen Fae were bringing food and drink to the injured who were able to eat.

The injured Fae were mostly sitting at tables eating and drinking. Looking pale and exhausted, dark circles under their eyes. Tuuli took a quick count. There must have been about four hundred of them.

Most of them were sylphs, but not all. Some were water, earth and fire Fae.

The really badly injured ones were laid out on other tables with healers surrounding them. There were probably twenty of the badly injured.

She spotted Aura at one of the tables, conferring with

Meredith about a Fae who had ridden back on Keirosum. That Fae hadn't woken up at all during the long ride back to Faerie.

Aidan stood talking with Egan and Pearce and a few other stone and fire Fae. They were all grinning. As they should be. They had gotten all the sylphs out. And everyone had made it back.

As far as Tuuli could tell, she was the only sylph whose wings had been taken. All the others were intact, although some were terribly bruised, beaten or starved. Her heart wept for the pain they had gone through. Tuuli wished there was some way she could help them.

But she'd done everything she could.

And she felt tired.

One of the kitchen Fae handed her a mug of hot mead.

"No thank you."

"Aura said to make sure you drink this. And that you eat something."

Tuuli sighed. She took the mug and the offered pastry.

"Drink," said the kitchen Fae. Who obviously was going to stand there to make sure she obeyed.

Tuuli sighed again and sipped the warm mead. The sweet wine was very comforting. She swallowed, feeling its heat travel down her throat and then permeate her whole body. She took a bite of the pastry filled with sweet berries and a creamy cheese. It tasted rich and decadent. And filled her with a sense of safety and well being.

She finished both, while the kitchen Fae stood and waited. Then she handed the empty mug back to her and licked her fingers.

"Thank you," she said.

"You are welcome. Now you are supposed to go to bed. The

healer will come see you in the morning, unless you are injured.”

“No, I am fine. Just tired.”

“Go to bed then. And sleep well knowing that you helped save many Fae tonight.”

With that the Fae returned to the kitchen.

The mead had made Tuuli feel even more tired.

She left the room and climbed the stairs to the second floor. Her legs felt heavy and it was all she could do to make it to the top.

Inside her room, Tuuli pulled off the heavy boots and fur clothes. Beneath those were the soft tunic and shirt she’d worn. She removed those and slipped into the pool of warm water that sat in the room.

The water felt heavenly and she sat in it for quite a bit. Her back ached, the wounds where her wings had been attached. Sadness filled her.

Tuuli cried for a long time, mingling her salty tears with the pool water. She hoped salt water was healing for her back, because there was plenty of it.

Now, more than ever, she didn’t belong among the air Fae. Not without wings. Before there had been only two others, Aura and Skye. And Skye wasn’t even here. It had been easier to ignore the fact she didn’t belong.

But now, there were hundreds.

She had no family any more. She couldn’t even go to the sylphs sleeping quarters. High in the cliffs. She couldn’t fly to get there.

She’d lost everything important.

At some point while sitting in the pool feeling sorry for herself, the water had grown cold. Then it drained out.

Even the pool was kicking her out.

She dried herself and climbed into the bed, pulling the covers up and hoping for good dreams at least.

Perhaps she'd wake in the morning to find her wings had returned. That the past couple of seasons had all been a bad dream. And that everything was the way that it should be.

But she didn't really believe it.

CHAPTER 16 ~ ADAIRE

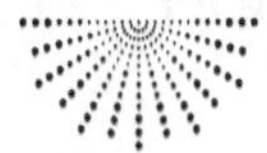

"Adaire," Fiachna said.

Adaire stirred slightly, having slept deeply in the mossy hollow of the tree. She snuggled deeper into the oak.

She was wearing fur. Why was that?

She tried to remember.

She'd been having a dream about flying. And she was wearing fur and talking with her friend, Ethelgarde. A beautiful, opalescent dragon.

Had the world turned upside down?

"Adaire," Fiachna called, again.

She opened her eyes.

It was midday. Her body told her she'd been sleeping for days. In the same position. She could smell the damp humous scent of the earth that the tree grew in, the woody fragrance of its bark. She could almost taste the rich soil that sustained the oak's roots. The moss felt soft against her face. For just a moment, Adaire was tempted to fall back asleep.

She was home, everything was well.

But the forest was awake and alive. Birds twittered and flitted between tree branches and the ground. The weather had warmed a bit more. It must be nearly spring. Everything felt more alive.

Then it came to her. The air Fae were back.

And Faerie was celebrating.

"Adaire," Fiachna called, for the third time.

"I'm here!"

She heard him coming. Stone Fae weren't the quietest.

Adaire stood in one fluid motion, only hampered by the heavy boots.

She should return these winter clothes to the palace.

Fiachna appeared on the deer trail which cut through the oak grove.

"Good morning," she said.

"Afternoon," he said. "We have been looking for you."

"I was sleeping."

"For three days?"

"I've been sleeping for three days?"

"Yes. It is time to come back to life. Meredith and Ogden are worried about you."

"Why?"

"Because no Fae has seen you since you landed on whatever island you landed on. We can't find anyone who knew if you were alive, wounded or left behind."

"I was so tired. I needed quiet. So I came here to sleep. I didn't mean to worry anyone."

"So come to the palace and show the elders that you are fine. Then you can return here and sleep if you want."

"All right. I have to return all these furs anyway. It's much too warm for here in the forest."

They walked down the deer trail towards the palace.

Beneath the great trees, bulbs had begun to come up. Small white bell flowers were open.

"The snowdrops are open. I missed Imbolc didn't I?"

"The fire festival was last night."

How could she have missed the first stirrings of spring? She was a dryad, she should have felt it. It hit her then, how exhausted she must be.

So, how are things?" she asked.

"The sylphs are back. And most of them are healing quickly. A few aren't. Perhaps never will. But most of Faerie is content. Except for the Fomorians continually trying to break through the barriers."

"You want this war to be over, don't you? You miss Claire and want to return to her."

"Yes. I do not know how I will like living in the human world. It will be very different. But I miss her so very much. And humans live such short lives. I hate that I am missing even a moment of hers."

Adaire nodded. It must be awful for him.

"Do you think we'll ever find a way to defeat them?"

"I do not know. I am not very hopeful about that. We have tried everything we could think of."

"What about that idea of Meredith's? About the mead?"

He snorted.

"I do not think our bees can make that much mead. I also see no reason why the Fomorians will drink it. It is not that simple."

"I wish it was," said Adaire.

"I do too. I really do."

They were silent the rest of the way.

The deer trail led to a wider path and then to a stone walkway through the formal gardens filled with boxwood and herbs. The sun blasted down and Adaire removed the fur coat.

They crossed the road, where she'd last seen Ethelgarde. The entire plaza was empty.

The palace had created an extension which jutted out over the half of the wide stairs. The new section had wall to wall windows, supported with sturdy marble columns that ran from the stairs beneath the extension to the ceiling. The whole thing looked light and airy from the outside. The entrance must be in the throne room.

Adaire suspected it was where the badly injured sylphs were staying.

They climbed the stairs. Adaire's stomach growled and her mouth felt dry. It had been so long since she'd eaten and drank anything.

They entered the palace. Adaire laid the fur coat on a bench near the front entrance. She removed the boots and deerskin pants and left them there too. With her bare feet, light pants and shirt, she felt more awake.

More like herself.

The carved wooden ceiling of the throne room arched over the crowd of Fae. Many of them were eating, others standing or sitting and listening to the Council.

Fiachna held onto her hand and pulled her past the tables and through the crowd to the front of the throne room.

Adaire saw the Council of Luminaries were having a discussion with two sylphs.

Aura said, "Skeeter, I understand your intentions were noble, although thoughtless. I hope this had taught you something."

"It has. I am never leaving Faerie again," the young Fae said. He looked pale with dark circles under his eyes.

Much like Tuuli had when she first arrived. Adaire felt badly about not even having asked Fiachna about the sylph. She had wanted to. But part of her felt if she didn't mention her, if she ignored her existence, than the desire to be with her would go away.

Aura said to Skeeter, "That isn't exactly what I meant. I expect the two of you to spend most of the next few days in the healing room, doing whatever the healers require of you. Helping those who are still injured in part because of your decision to leave Faerie without consulting the Luminary. No one even knew where you were. We will speak again, later."

"Thank you," they said, bowing in unison and fleeing to the healers' room.

Fiachna pulled Adaire forwards, bowed and left.

"Adaire, it is good to see you healthy and alive," said Ogden. "We feared the worst."

"I was just so exhausted that I curled up with a tree, and slept until Fiachna woke me."

"Well, I am pleased you are safe. And thank you for your part in this rescue. If you, Egan and Pearce had not gone, we might not have gotten everyone returned safely. It is good to have nearly everyone back," said Meredith.

"Nearly everyone?" asked Adaire.

"I think we must bring Skye and Kian back. They are not safe out in the world with so many Fomorians loose. They never were. But we are afraid they might become a target now," said Meredith.

"I'm sorry to hear that," said Adaire. "She loves her work so much."

Meredith said, "I realize that. We also need her healing powers here. The only really skilled healer of the air elementals is Aura. She is not enough. She's completely worn out and there's only so much those of us other elements can do."

"What happened to the other air healers?"

"Five of them are in that room near death," said Meredith, pointing towards the healers' room. Aura says they probably burned themselves out, trying to keep the others alive. They had no food, water or fresh air to revitalize themselves."

"How many were rescued?"

"Over four hundred. A surprising amount of them were Water, Earth and Fire Fae."

"I hadn't realized there were that many. So much of the rescue was done in the dark."

She hesitated, then asked, "Was there a reason you wanted to see me? Other than to make sure I was all right?"

"Yes," said Meredith, taking her arm and walking towards the kitchen with her. When they were alone in a passageway, she said, "We're worried about Tuuli. She isn't mingling with the other sylphs."

"Why should she? Sylphs are often solitary."

"Aura says Tuuli isn't."

"Being held prisoner and tortured is bound to have changed her."

"Yes, but Aura thinks it's more than that. She's very worried and she has enough on her mind."

Adaire was silent for a minute, then said, "I suspect Tuuli's depressed. She's had her wings ripped off. Or cut off. She's lost her element. Why would she want to mingle with the others? She doesn't belong there anymore."

"Exactly. We think you're her best hope for recovery."

"I'm not sure what I can do," said Adaire.

"Be with her. It's not good for her to be so alone."

"I was with her the night she disappeared, remember. That didn't work out so well."

"It did though. Without Tuuli they might never have found the tunnel and gotten all the Fae out. But that's another story. She needed to go back and take part in the rescue. We should have seen that. What we're seeing now is that she needs help," said Meredith

"I'll do what I can. I'm not sure how much that is though." There was no way to get around this. She was going to just have to deal with her attraction to Tuuli. To let it go. It wouldn't be right to let Tuuli know, not when the sylph was so down.

"Thank you. And please let us know how she's doing. I want Aura to have less to worry about."

"You mean report in to you."

"Unfortunately, that's exactly what I mean. I'm worried about her too."

"I'll see what I can do," said Adaire. Although she didn't like the idea of gossiping, she understood their fears. "Where is Tuuli now?"

"She hasn't left her room, since she returned."

"Is she awake?"

"Aura spoke with her. So, yes. But she is exhausted, the healer said. Her back is still not completely healed."

"I'll go see her."

"Please eat something first. Take care of yourself, too."

"I will," said Adaire. She really was hungry. Especially standing outside the kitchen and smelling the soup that was being made for dinner.

She went out towards a table and picked up a berry scone from a platter of leftover pastries from breakfast. The blackberries were tart and the scone, bready and flavorful. She munched on it as she walked up the stairs to Tuuli's room.

Adaire knocked on Tuuli's door. There was no answer.

"Tuuli, it's Adaire. Are you there?"

A couple of minutes later the door cracked open.

"Adaire?"

"Hi. Are you okay?"

Tuuli opened the door and Adaire walked in.

The room smelled stuffy. Air Fae didn't usually like stuffy places.

It was also dark, with heavy curtains pulled over the window.

"You're not okay," said Adaire.

Tuuli plunked down on a chair.

"No. I guess you could say I am doing badly."

"Why?" asked Adaire.

She sat on a chair next to Tuuli.

"I no longer belong anywhere. I do not belong in Faerie. I am no longer air, but also not earth or water or fire either. I do not belong in the world outside Faerie either. I belong nowhere."

Adaire said, slowly, "I understand some of what you're feeling. I didn't have my wings torn off, no. But when I returned to Faerie after being imprisoned and escaping, I didn't fit in. That's one of the reasons I left in the first place. I've never fit in. I didn't believe what other Fae did. That Faerie should be closed to the world. And living with humans for so long, didn't leave me having anything in common with other Fae. I still feel solitary. I have made my own place in Faerie. That is what you'll have to do. Make your own life."

"I do not know how to do that."

"Well, it won't happen overnight. And it won't be easy. And

no one can really tell you how to do it. That's something you'll have to figure out yourself."

"And how do I do that?"

"By getting up every morning and going outside. Faerie is more than this palace and the Fae who live here. She is the land, the creatures who walk, swim and fly. She is the water that streams through the earth, the air that blows past. You must begin to live again."

"I feel so ashamed of myself. Feeling so sorry for myself, when there are sylphs down there in much worse shape than me. Some burned so badly their skin will never heal. Others with mangled arms and legs, that might never go right again. Sylphs are supposed to be beautiful. There are Fae who are worth a hundred of me. Fae who are stronger and more powerful."

"Other being's pain does not negate your own. And I don't believe that any one Fae is better than any other. I believe we are all equal. Some of us younger, some older. Some more skilled in one area, some in others. But equal."

"I wish I believed that."

"It's hard when you're going through a rough patch. Come on. Have you eaten today?"

"Yes, the healer brought up food and put salve on my back."

"Well, then let's go for a walk. It's a glorious day outside."

Tuuli gave her a dubious look.

"It is. Spring isn't here yet, but the buds on trees are swelling. The fullness of spring is out there to be seen. One must only look. New life is just around the bend."

Tuuli grudgingly stood, then slipped on a pair of dark blue pants and a lighter blue shirt. She put a pair of leather shoes on and tied them.

Then looked in the mirror and tried to flatten her spiky hair to no avail.

"Okay, let's go."

They went down the stairs and on their way out of the palace, Adaire grabbed two more pastries from the throne room, giving one to Tuuli.

Tuuli took it and sighed, as if resigned to being ordered about.

They went out the big double doors of the palace, Adaire bent on finding something that would pique Tuuli's interest.

CHAPTER 17 ~ TUULI

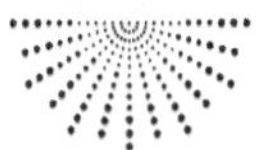

TUULI SAT ON A HARD WOODEN CHAIR IN HER GAUZY blue room and laced up the sturdy leather boots. Her fingers were clumsy this morning, getting stuck in the laces. She was trying to hurry, so eager to go.

She tugged her long sleeved blue shirt into place. She'd worn dark, brown leather pants so she'd stay warm enough.

This was the third day in a row that the secretive dryad was dragging her out into the world.

Today, Tuuli was excited to go.

It was a glorious day out, sunny, but probably crisp. The sun hung low in the winter sky and blasted in through the window, its light blinding.

She stood, her belly pleasantly full from a breakfast of sausages, biscuits and gravy. The food had tasted as rich and hearty as the intense scent had promised.

Tuuli knelt down and dipped her head in the pool, rubbing water all over her hair. Then she dried it off with a fluffy towel. In front of the ancient mottled mirror, she brushed her hair down with her fingers, trying to get the dark spikes to lie down. Most of it did.

Sylphs didn't get dirty, but their hair sometimes needed taming. Especially, when it was short. And hers hadn't been this short since she'd been a child. Most sylphs, most Fae, just let their hair grow as long as it would. It was common to have hair fall past the knees. Except for Fire Fae, who were often bald and scaled.

Tuuli looked out the window, there was no signs of the dragons yet. She paced around and around the small room, waiting for Adaire.

They'd eaten breakfast together and the dryad had gone to dress for the ride. They were going to ride the dragons to the old dragon caves with Dylan.

Tuuli felt so anxious.

Would Keirosum come?

She longed to see him again. She had loved flying with him.

The room seemed confining, too small. Perhaps it was time she moved out of the palace. Found another place to live. She felt sure that this room could be used by one of the newly returned Fae.

Adaire lived in the forest. Perhaps she could help Tuuli find a spot. An unoccupied cave? Or perhaps Tuuli could build a house, out of freshly downed logs. There were many at the edges of Faerie, Adaire said. Places where the trees had been killed by the war.

The knock on the door startled her. Tuuli was almost instantly at the door, opening it.

"Ready?" asked Adaire.

"Yes," said Tuuli, coming out and closing the door behind her.

"You're eager this morning."

"I am. I have missed Keirosum."

"Ah, I understand. I've missed Ethelgarde. Dragons are fascinating."

They walked down the stairs quickly.

Tuuli was surprised that Adaire missed Ethelgarde. She'd tried to explain her own feelings to Aura, who just didn't understand.

"I had no idea they could send."

"I had never sent before, so it was a shock to me," said Tuuli.

"And you had no problems sending with the dragon?"

"No. No one had ever tried to teach me before that."

Dylan came out of the throne room with his pack of painting supplies.

Tuuli grabbed a heavy knitted brown wool sweater off a hook and put it on. She pulled a green wool hat on her head and carried a pair of leather gloves.

Adaire and Dylan put on outer wear as well. Dylan opting for a thin leather coat. Then they went out the palace doors and stood under the shelter of the eaves, so as not to be blown down when the dragons came.

They heard the dragons before they saw them. One by one, three dragons landed. Tuuli recognized Spike and Ethelgarde.

Her heart leapt when Keirosum landed.

"*Keirosum,*" she said, before he had even slowed to a stop.

Once the dragons were all down, Tuuli and the others went out into the courtyard.

Tuuli ran to his head, hugging his nose and mouth. He gave his rasping laugh.

"It is good to see you, little one."

"I've missed you so much."

"It has only been six days."

"Is that all? It seems like years. What have you been doing?"

"Preparing for the move," he said.

"What move?"

"The Council have agreed to let us all return to Faerie. To live. So we are digging new caverns. Our population has expanded some since we left."

"You are going to live inside Faerie? That is exciting."

"We are pleased. We dragons use up so much of our energy trying to stay invisible to humans that we have little for anything else. It is exhausting to maintain vigilance all the time. In Faerie we will be able to have a sanctuary, again. Which means we will be able to save our strength, using those powers for when we leave Faerie, to hunt for food."

"That means I will be able to see more of you," said Tuuli.

"We are honored to carry you and each of us has created our own rigging so there will always be enough of them to go around," said Keirosum. "We value your company so much. You teach us so much. We dragons have been alone for far too long. It is time we lived in the world again."

She began climbing up the rigging and tied herself in. Dylan and Adaire were already up.

"I have missed you so. I do not have many friends. I want to spend more time with the ones I have," said Tuulli.

"But you sylphs are always the most sought out of Fae. Or so I always heard. Sylphs are always the center of attention, the best at making friends, the most beautiful."

Spike began his run across the courtyard and took off over the stairs.

"But I do not fit in any more," she sent.

"Because the Fomorians took your wings."

"Yes. I cannot fly to the cliffs where the sylphs live. And to have to

climb up there would only be pathetic. They already look at me with such pity. I want my friends to feel joyful around me, not be sad."

"But you are sad. How can we not be sad with you?"

"I don't know," sent Tuuli.

Ethelgarde took off. He was so large that Tuuli could feel the earth vibrate as he ran. By the time Keirosum took off, people had come out of the palace to watch.

They soared over one of the great oak forests of Faerie. Tuuli loved the feel of the wind flowing past. It felt glorious.

Tears streamed down her cheeks.

Keirosum sent, *"There is such sadness in you. You miss flying, am I right?"*

"I do. I miss it terribly. This feels wonderful. The only thing better would be to have my own wings. I used to fly all the time, I rarely walked anywhere if I could fly. I have lost the most precious part of myself."

"Then we must fly more often," he said.

She had no idea what would heal her. Give her a reason to live.

Spike wove between tall pines and headed down a valley, following the path of a stream. Every place they flew Tuuli recognized from the air.

The valley was where she and Skeeter used to race. That meant they were fairly close to where the sylphs lived. Close to her old home.

Home.

That was part of the problem. She no longer had one.

CHAPTER 18 ~ ADAIRE

Adaire felt very comfortable riding on Ethelgarde. The fresh smelling cold wind whipping past, the heat of his body beneath her. His smooth, polished scales underneath her hands. His wings were thunderously loud, except when he soared. Which felt so very natural to her.

She'd spent all her life avoiding that part of her. Her father had been a dryad and her mother a sylph. And Adaire had been born without wings, so it was obvious she should be a dryad. Yet, she'd always felt a certain restlessness about her. Not like other dryads who often paired with a tree and often grew into them. Rarely leaving their tree, and even more rarely, the forest.

Not many dryads had left Faerie when it closed. When she'd gone to live in the human world it had been easy to ignore that she didn't really fit in with the dryads, much as Tuuli didn't feel at home with the sylphs anymore. Adaire had been a stranger, among strangers.

What she'd told Tuuli, about feeling like she didn't have a place in Faerie after being imprisoned, wasn't strictly the truth.

Adaire had always felt that way. Except when Ashleigh had been alive.

Ethelgarde rose higher and Adaire leaned into the chilled air that battered her face. She could almost taste the end of winter on it. The season was fighting a battle to stay, but down below, in the earth, spring was coming. Buds swelled, green shoots of the first bulbs, snowdrops, crocus and daffodils, were coming up.

Spring would not be held back.

The dragon dove, following Spike down a narrow valley and then swooped up the side of a mountain, losing speed just enough so that he landed with only three steps before stopping on a flat ledge.

Moments later, Keirosum landed beside him.

The ledge was wide and deep enough for about six dragons to land, side by side. The mouth of the cave, was about five large dragons wide, but the inside was simply immense. There were a few smaller rooms off the main one, where there was space for many dragons.

From what Adaire had learned, the dragons liked living in one large room together. The back rooms were a bit warmer and the eggs were laid there. Large chunks of wood were brought in to keep a fire burning for the eggs to stay warm.

Adaire unstrapped herself and climbed down.

"That was lovely, my friend."

"I'm please you enjoyed it. You are no longer afraid to fly?"

"Not with you."

Ethelgarde's scales glowed a bit more green. She'd noticed it happened when he was pleased. During the flight to rescue the sylphs he'd been bluish with worry. Then he'd turned red. Barely able to keep his rage controlled.

Mostly he was ivory colored, with all the other colors subtly glimmering beneath the surface of his scales.

He reminded her of an opal she'd once seen. It had contained all the colors in the rainbow, whichever one was showing depended on the light.

Adaire walked farther into the cave following Dylan and Tuuli. She'd never been there, even as a child. The sylphs lived nearby, but apparently this had held no interest for her.

It did now. Dylan showed her various paintings done by the dragons.

The light slanted in sideways, illuminating most of the cave, because the sun was still low in the sky. But during high summer the cave would be darkish, and cool.

The entire cave was covered in designs in a rainbow of colors, some bright, some very subtle. Red foxes hid behind green bushes covered with wild, pink roses. Yellow birds flitted between green-gray pine needled branches. Light brown hares streaked across fields of yellowing grass. Bluish water wove through dark brown mud to a greenish-gray sea with whitecaps on the tips of waves.

The paintings were as complex as the world they depicted. No creature was too small to paint. Dragons clearly registered the presence of bees and ants as well as larger animals like stags with massive sets of antlers.

Adaire stood and stared at the walls, everything looked so real. Yew trees looked like they should, down to minute details like the gnarled branches. Hawthorns had deeply grooved bark. She could almost smell the sweetness of the fragrant heath orchid. The small pink-purple blossoms so lovingly painted.

Dylan was putting wood and dried brush into a fire pit in the center of the cave. There were several such pits in the large cave. Once he had it piled high, he stepped back and Spike flamed it, setting everything alight.

The glow from the fire showed even more details in the paintings. Tuuli walked along the wall, her mouth open in wonder.

Keirosum and Ethelgarde stood gazing at the walls and ceiling.

"I could never tire of looking at this," said Ethelgarde.

"When you all move back in here, what will you do? There is no more space to paint," said Adaire.

"We will redo the parts that are fading. And that's one of the reason we are digging deeper into the mountain, finding more caves," said Keirosum.

"Not all dragons are artists," said Ethelgarde. "Some of us are storytellers, others nurture the young. There are many roles in our weir. These caves were painted over many, many generations of dragons. We lived here since the beginning of time."

"I'm sorry you were forced to leave," Adaire said.

"Leaving made us appreciate our home even more. And I believe we had grown callous in our treatment of the other beings we shared this world with. That is never a good thing."

Tuuli came over and said, "I had no idea this existed."

Tears were streaming down her face.

Adaire hugged her. Tuuli put an arm around Adaire's waist.

Adaire's first instinct was to stiffen and pull away, but she didn't allow herself to. She just let that gesture be, as she listened to Tulli's awe about the paintings.

"That dragonfly, look at the detail. How you can see the veining in the transparent wings. Dragonflies are so delicate, yet so fierce at the same time."

Dylan had set up his easel and pulled out a canvas. He was painting, copying a section that showed a dragon with a butterfly on its nose. And a badger sitting at its feet.

It didn't have the cutesy look that much human art would, using the same subject matter. And he painted the wall, on his canvas, where it joined the floor. So it was made clear that it was a painting of a painting.

It was then that Adaire looked at the floor of the cave. It was mostly covered with layers of dirt and debris that had blown in. But the area where Dylan was painting had been swept, revealing the intricate design covering the floor. It looked like Celtic knot work and covered the space he'd cleared.

Did it extend to the entire cave floor?

Adaire pulled a stiff pine branch that still held green needles from the firewood pile. She began moving the dust and debris, broken branches and twigs. Tuuli found another branch and helped sweep dirt away, beginning close to where the cave floor met the wall.

Ethelgarde and Keirosum watched and then began using their great tails to scrape debris off the edge of the cliff.

The two Fae took breaks between cleaning, peeling off the warm flying clothes as they worked.

It took till long after the sun reached its peak in the sky, but eventually they had the entire floor cleared. And every bit of it had been painted in the same manner. The colors had faded with age and wear, but the design was still clear.

"We will need to get this fully cleaned and repainted before we move in," said Ethelgarde.

Dylan said, "I suspected the painting went farther out, but not that it covered the cave floor as well."

"How did you dragons get the floor so smooth and flat?" asked Tuuli.

"Some of us are stoneworkers," said Spike. "They probably carved it to be almost smooth and then polished it."

"Perhaps a generation or two of dragon feet helped with that," said Keirosum.

"Yes, the caves we live in now, outside of Faerie, are still being smoothed. We have done no painting on the floors," said Ethelgarde.

Even the dragons seemed astonished at finding the floor.

As the sun was setting, Dylan packed up and they flew back to the palace.

Adaire felt tired and dirty. She liked being dirty, but usually it was from the moist earth beneath trees, not decades of dry dust. Rain and snow hadn't make it far into the cave, despite the large opening.

At the palace, the dragons landed and Adaire and the others climbed off.

Tuuli seemed very tired. Adaire hoped she hadn't overdone it.

The days were gradually getting longer, spring would be coming soon.

They said goodbye to the dragons and walked inside.

The Fae removed their warm clothes and lay them on benches inside the door.

They washed up in a large pool with a fountain that stood inside the main entrance. The water was brown with dust before it drained off, replaced with fresh, clear water. Had the fountain been there this morning? Adaire didn't think so.

She took a towel and dried off.

In the throne room, she heard raised voices and went inside

to get some food and to see what was happening. Tuuli and Dylan followed.

The room was jammed with people.

She could hear, but not see Meredith. "We have no choice. We must act. Now. Before they are lost."

Alana said, "I will risk no more Stone Faes' lives. We have lost too many of our people already."

CHAPTER 19 ~ TUULI

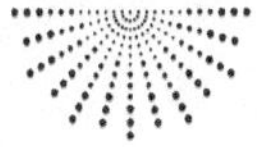

Tuuli stepped into the throne room. It was filled with sylphs. Many of them were fluttering about the ceiling worriedly.

How long since she had seen sylphs flying around the throne room?

Other Fae filled the floor of the great room. It seemed too packed for anything other than a festival or a major event.

Something important must have happened.

The smell of too many bodies in too small a space was overwhelming. Every Fae had their own scent, many were like perfumed flowers, others smelled like various stones. Still others like rain or green grass. Also, the smoke from the four different fires weren't escaping as well as it usually did.

The complex tapestries on the wall flapped, perhaps from the breeze caused by all the sylphs' wings, perhaps from exasperation. The patterns on individual tapestries kept changing, as if they couldn't decide what the history of Faerie should be.

Adaire had worked her way along the side of the room where it wasn't as crowded. Tuuli followed in her wake.

The room felt burning hot from all the bodies and the emotion.

They passed the front table, where no one was sitting. Tuuli grabbed a scone as she went by. The pastry had biting ginger in it, which made her mouth feel as hot as the room.

Dylan followed behind.

They were close enough now to see the Council.

A fire Fae stood in front of them. Tuuli didn't recognize him. He looked dirty and worn, as if he'd been living rough. And cold. His arms wrapped around himself.

The council didn't seem to be paying much attention to him. They were arguing among themselves.

"Someone's got to go to England," said Meredith.

"No they don't," said Aura. "They might not be in danger. The Fomorians might not find them. After all Skye's in a human body."

"Kian is not," said Ogden. "He merely disguises his antlers. He would still glow enough to attract their attention."

"To go retrieve them would be foolish. We might lose everyone who went."

Adaire whispered to an earth Fae in front of her, "What's happening?"

The Fae said, "He, the fire Fae, overheard one of the Fomorians, the earthquake, speaking to a wind. The earthquake said he knew where two other Fae were. Across the narrow water. He pointed to the east. The wind said he'd go find them. Now the Council are arguing whether to go rescue those two Fae."

Adaire nodded, her hands clenching into fists.

Tuuli's belly clenched with fear.

"It may already be too late," said Conley. "The wind could be there already."

"He may not know where to find them," said Meredith.

Adaire stepped forward, pushing through the crowd. Tuuli followed where the crowd parted. Dylan did the same.

"I'll go," said Adaire. "Faerie wouldn't be here if it wasn't for Skye. We wouldn't have made it back to warn anyone about the Fomorians. They would have destroyed everything." Adaire gestured around the room.

Tuuli stood on the edge of the crowd now. She'd sucked in a breath of air.

Adaire was so brave.

It was if Tuuli saw her clearly for the first time.

Meredith was staring at Adaire.

"I think we need someone who's stronger, my dear. One of the Fire Fae, who's a fast runner," Meredith said.

"I'm strong enough. I'll ask Ethelgarde to take me. It'll be faster."

Tuuli stood up straighter. She could do that.

Adaire's courage made her feel stronger.

"I will go too. Keirosum will take me. We can carry both of them back safely," Tuuli said.

Meredith looked astonished.

Aura stood up and said, "No. You have been through too much already."

Tuuli bowed and said, "I respect your opinion, but I have nothing to do here. I cannot fly on my own anymore. I do not belong with the sylphs. The only way I can fly is with a dragon. So let me fly. Let me be useful."

Aura stood looking at her, as if reappraising her.

"I'll go too," said Egan.

"I will too," said Dylan.

"I will go as well," said Fiachna.

Meredith sank down into her chair, putting a hand over her face.

"Very well," said Alana. "I will sanction this rescue if all the other elements are included. But you must return, Fiachna. As long as we are at war with the Fomorians, none of us is safe outside of Faerie. You would only endanger your human lover."

He bowed at her.

"Then it is settled," said Conley.

"Someone tell the kitchen to get food ready to take along," said Aura.

"You five get changed into warm clothes. And can someone call the dragons?" asked Meredith.

"I'll call them," said Tuuli.

She sent a message to Keirosum.

"Will you, Ethelgarde, Spike and two other dragons come. We need to fly across the sea to collect two more Fae. The Fomorians are going to attack them. Take them prisoner or kill them. We might have trouble."

"We will come," he sent back. *"Now?"*

"Now."

Tuuli followed the others out into the hallway. Apparently, the palace had already cleaned and folded their recently used warm clothes.

As she dressed in deerskin pants and a heavy wool sweater, Tuuli searched her feelings. Did she really want to do this?

She felt afraid, yes. But determined to push through the fear. The Fomorians terrified her. But the thought of Adaire and Keirosum going along on the journey gave her strength.

She could do this.

Rescuing two Fae who weren't being held prisoner seemed easier than rescuing hundreds of Fae in cold iron cages. And

Skye, Skye was a legend. The sylph who'd gone out into the human world and returned. Much like Adaire.

Although there might be several Fomorians there already.

She shook off the fear and laced up leather boots.

Two Earth Fae came from the kitchen with food for them to take. She took one basket and Dylan took another.

There was a thundering sound outside.

The dragons were here.

CHAPTER 20 ~ ADAIRE

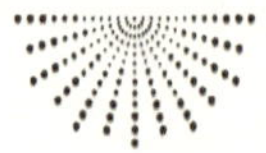

ADAIRE MOVED TOWARDS ETHELGARDE IN THE courtyard as soon as he landed and stopped running. She hugged his smooth scaled snout.

"Thank you for coming, my friend."

"I am honored to help you do anything, my friend. Where are we going?"

"Across the sea again, to England. Glastonbury."

She pictured the route in her mind and sent it to him.

"I understand."

Adaire climbed up the rigging and strapped herself in.

The other four had already strapped in and the dragons were getting ready to take off. Their muscles bunched, heads down.

The first dragon, was smaller than Ethelgarde, who was the largest. It was ridden by Fiachna. The dragon was a rusty brown with a line of spiked protrusions on the back of its long neck and tail. Adaire hadn't seen that dragon before. It began the takeoff run, lumbering along. Fiachna's face had a look of surprise on it. Adaire knew he had never ridden a dragon before.

Ethelgarde took off last. She spotted several riderless dragons flying in circles high above them.

Were they coming too?

By the time they topped the tree line, the last glimmers of sunlight were dropping below the horizon, and darkness settled in.

The clear sky shone with stars. She could see the constellations which formed the battle where Nuada lost his arm. And Danu giving birth to all her children at once. Faerie's ancestors still going on with their lives, only now they were up in the wild stretches of the universe.

Looking behind, Adaire saw that the riderless dragons were indeed coming along. Probably to help if there were Fomorians about.

That made her feel more courageous. It was more difficult to conjure up fear when your allies were dragons. But the Fomorians were formidable. It worried her that no one had found a way to defeat them yet.

Hours later, they flew over the Irish Sea. The dragons with riders were flying nearby, although she couldn't see them clearly in the darkness. The stars were covered with heavy clouds and cold rain poured down on them as if someone had forgotten to turn the tap off. Even through the sealskin coat she wore, Adaire felt drenched. And it was full dark.

Why did they always seem to be flying in the dark?

Adaire shivered from the cold wetness and shifted in the rigging. She tucked her hands into the deep pockets of the coat.

Down below, she could just barely see a large boat with lots of lights being tossed in the waves. Maybe a ferry.

The wind streamed past her face. She didn't know if there

were any Fomorians out there or not, it was too dark to see them if they were there. She couldn't sense them either.

She opened her mouth and sipped some of the fresh rain. Quenching her thirst. And shifted in the rigging a bit again.

"Are you all right?"

"Fine. Just stiff. And wet. And cold."

"We will be there in a while."

"Not soon enough."

She could sense Ethelgarde's amusement.

After what seemed like several more hours, Adaire could see a line of lights. It must be the coast of England ahead.

They were getting close.

At least they'd lost the rain somewhere over the sea.

She sent to Skye, *"Skye, are you there? Wake up. Skye."*

Several minutes later she sent the same message.

"Who are you?"

"It's Adaire."

"Where are you?"

"Just about to England. We'll be there soon. Meet us at the Tor. Both you and Kian. And Clare, I think. There may be Fomorians, be careful."

"Why are you here?"

"To take you and Kian back to Faerie. It's no longer safe for you here."

"Damn."

"I know. But it has to happen."

"Why Clare?" asked Skye.

"Fiachna's with us. But he can't stay."

"How are we going back?"

"Dragons."

"What?"

"We're flying on dragons. Don't worry, you'll like it."

"We'll be there."

At least the wind was blowing them towards shore quickly. She hoped it would change direction on their way back.

Adaire sent to Tuuli, Dylan, Egan and Fiachna, *"We should cast a glamour of invisibility over ourselves. Our glow might attract any Fomorians."*

She pulled a veil of nothingness over herself. Anyone looking at her would see nothing. The dragons would do the same when they got inland. But they weren't targets of the Fomorians. They didn't glow like Fae did.

And she didn't want to make a human body to hide in. It would make her too slow and dull her senses and her power.

It took roughly four more hours to reach Glastonbury Tor. Dawn was near, but it still looked fairly dark. She hoped there weren't a lot of sunrise watchers out. Or Fomorians. Adaire believed Fomorians sensed Fae by smell or their other senses, not just by seeing them.

Adaire couldn't see where the other dragons were, but she could hear their wings. Perhaps Ethelgarde had taken the lead.

He flew around the tall, grassy hill, the Tor. Which was topped by the ruins of an old church. The only remaining tower stuck up from the top of the hill. An eyesore to the Fae, who preferred trees. The hill was terraced and there were paths up from the bottom. She was too far away to feel Skye, Kian or Clare.

"Skye are your there?"

"We're halfway up."

Adaire still couldn't see them. Perhaps they were invisible.

"We'll land at the top."

Adaire passed the message to Tuuli and the others. The dragons landed one by one, obviously they knew where the others were.

Adaire climbed down the rigging. She could see beneath

the glamour as if Ethelgarde was underneath a blanket. But once she was on the ground and walked away, he was invisible.

"Can you and the other dragons lighten your invisibility a little, so we can see your outlines and not run into you?"

"Certainly," said Ethelgarde.

He became a barely, visible shadow. So did the other dragons.

Dylan, Egan and Tuuli stayed on their dragons to wait. Only she and Fiachna got down.

She heard lightly running footsteps and then heavy breathing.

Then sensed Kian. Followed by a herd of wild deer.

He lessened his invisibility a bit.

Adaire did the same and pointed to the dragons.

"Climb up and strap yourself on. We can't stay long."

Kian ran to Dylan's dragon and began to climb up.

Skye, and a human woman, who Adaire assumed was Clare, came next. Clare was slight with shoulder-length blondish hair. She was out of breath from running.

Adaire hugged Skye, who returned the hug.

Fiachna was embracing the human, and speaking to her softly.

Skye was in Fae form.

"Climb up on a dragon and strap yourself on. We might have to leave in a hurry."

"I can't ride a dragon."

"You must. It's a long flight and they're faster. Fomorians. Now hurry."

Skye sighed and looked warily at the dragons.

Adaire said, "C'mon, I'll introduce you to Ethelgarde. He's quite lovely."

"I don't understand any of this. I thought dragons were our enemies."

"It's a long story. I'll tell you as we ride."

She took Skye over to Ethelgarde, and introduced the dragon to her.

Skye said, "It's lovely to meet you."

"I've heard so much about you. Please climb up. I sense a Fomorian."

Skye began to climb the rigging.

"Fiachna. Trouble. Say goodbye."

He said, "I must take Clare somewhere away from here, safely."

"Well, climb aboard and let's get going. I don't know where you're going to take her. We need to get out of here and the Fomorian will follow us," said Adaire, climbing the rigging.

Fiachna helped Clare up the rusty, brown dragon and helped her strap in.

"You go," he said. "I will fly her down to her house and then catch up to you."

"How are you going to land in town?"

"We will find a place. It is early yet, most humans are not awake. Just go."

"You better come or the Council will have my hair."

"I will come," he said, grimly.

The dragons began to take off.

"Hang on," said Adaire to Skye, as Ethelgarde began to move.

He soared off the edge of the Tor just as the wind hit him in the chest.

Ethelgarde grunted and flapped his wings to get momentum. It didn't work and the wind blasted him backwards onto the ground. The dragon hit the side of the slope, but kept his feet beneath him. He ran around the side of the hill, startling Kian's herd of deer who fled out of the way.

The wind didn't feel normal. It was a Fomorian

The dragon was able to lift off on the other side and gain some height before the wind hit him again. This time Ethelgarde was prepared and used the gust to give him more altitude to fly above the wind's reach.

He sped through the air faster than Adaire had felt him fly before.

One of the rigging straps snapped. She was only held by the strap around her left leg.

Skye grabbed Adaire's arm before she could be blown off the dragon.

Adaire grabbed onto the remaining straps and pulled herself upright again.

Down below, five riderless dragons dove at the wind, pushing the Fomorian into the hill, blasting him with flames. The flames blew into a spiral of wind and the dragons held the whirling blaze in place with more fire.

"What's happening?" asked Ethelgarde.

"One of the straps broke," said Adaire.

"I'll stop and hover while you tie yourself back in, but hurry."

He slowed to a stop and slowed the beat of his wings, hovering in place.

Adaire moved over to another set of straps on the rigging, still leaving her one leg tied in and secured both legs and her hips with another set of straps.

"Go," she sent to Ethelgarde.

He beat his wings and dove a bit to gain speed, flying rapidly to catch up with the others.

Adaire saw the expression on Skye's face, a mixture of fear

and exhilaration. The sylph was enjoying the flying part, at least.

"*Fiachna, hurry,*" Adaire sent.

"*We are just over the town. Looking for a place to land.*"

Then Adaire sent to Ethelgarde, "*Can you ask the riderless dragons to keep him safe?*"

"*They already are. There are more of them than you can see. The ones attacking the Fomorian are just a small part of our escort.*"

Just before they made it to the coast Fiachna and the rust colored dragon caught up. Fiachna's face looked grim.

They were accompanied by at least ten riderless dragons.

And the Fomorian right behind, blowing them forward.

Into the fog.

Cethlenn.

CHAPTER 21 ~ TUULI

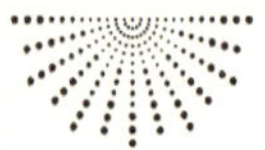

Tuuli looked ahead at the fog. She shuddered at the dense moistness of it. She'd heard tales of Cethlenn, the Fomorian. But Keirosum was flying so fast, being pushed from the wind behind.

There was no avoiding the fog.

"*Can you go around it?*" she asked Keirosum.

"*I can try to fly up through it. Up into the clouds. It is difficult to see where one ends and the other begins.*"

Keirosum began to fly upwards.

Tuuli could only hope the dragons could sense each other in the murkiness. As he moved farther into the fog, she could see nothing.

But she could feel everything. The dampness. The awful clammy fingers of the nasty giant. Her claws, Tuuli sensed the Fomorian was a her, grasped at Tuuli. Trying to pull her from the dragon.

Tuuli responded by sending a jolt of power into those grasping hands. They backed off, as if surprised by the attack. But the presence was still there, looking for an opening.

Tuuli constructed a field around herself and Keirosum. A shield of energy. And waited for the next attack.

Keirosum continued his climb upwards, his wings thundering all around her.

The fog grabbed at her again and Tuuli imagined herself as an agile kestrel, maneuvering out of the fog's grasp. Her hands tightened around the rigging, her throat closing in fear.

When the fog tightened its fingers again, Tuuli sent a raging wildfire down her arm and the fog retreated.

Shocked, Tuuli did it again, shooting fire out into the mist. The fog retreated farther.

Tuuli hadn't known she carried fire.

Keirosum finally slipped completely out of the fog and into the bank of low clouds. There was no difference in visibility, but the clouds felt natural, not nightmarish. They were a part of nature.

Unlike the fog, which felt wrong, unnatural, even though it was a fog. It was still a monster. A Fomorian.

She could hear muffled screaming.

"Can we go back and help?" she sent to Keirosum.

"No. I could see nothing in the fog, could you?"

"No."

Her heart sank. One of her friends was in trouble and she felt helpless.

She heard Keirosum send to the other dragons, *"Fly upwards. Out of the fog, up into the clouds."*

Tuuli hoped it was enough.

It seemed to take hours and hours as they sped forwards. Tuuli had no idea where they were, or if they were even flying in the right direction. Along with her wings she seemed to have lost her sense of direction.

Somewhere over the sea, the clouds vanished. The fog was

gone too.

Keirosum was the first to break through the clouds. Tuuli looked behind them. One by one dragons with riders came out of the cloud cover, until all five were there. Fiachna and his dragon lagged far behind the others.

She saw no sign of the riderless dragons for a very long time. The sun was low on the horizon behind them and it was difficult to see in that direction. The fog seemed to have disappeared and the sky was blindingly bright.

Hours later, they'd passed over the sea.

The green shores welcomed them. By then the riderless dragons had caught up to them. There were ten of them.

One of them was being carried by two other dragons. Its outspread wings resting on their tails, as if it couldn't fly on its own. They flew madly to catch up.

As they came closer Tuuli could see one of the dragons was holding a bloody back leg strangely. As if it was broken.

"*Have we lost anyone?*" she sent to Keirosum.

"*One dragon is missing.*"

"*Should we go back?*"

"*No, we can risk no more right now. We return to Faerie.*"

Tuuli took a deep breath and turned to look forward again. Faerie attempted rescues for their captured. Were dragons less important than Fae? Or perhaps Keirosum knew the missing dragon was dead. Or did dragons think differently about themselves? Did the life of a single dragon mean something different to dragons than a Fae life did to Fae?

She looked around at the dragons flying beside her. Tuuli hoped the missing dragon returned safely.

Adaire was looking straight ahead, her face grim, flying fairly close to Tuuli on the big ivory colored dragon. The sylph, Skye was looking around, her body unable to stay still.

It seemed another couple of hours before they flew through the boundary of Faerie. It felt strange, passing through it on a dragon. The speed was so fast, but it was like flying through a hundred spiderwebs at once. Sticky almost.

She felt relief as they penetrated the veil. Safe. They were home again.

The injured dragons landed in a large field a ways away from the palace. Had the dragons sent for their own healers or would they need help from the Fae? If they needed help, someone would have sent for them. Adaire perhaps?

Was that why she looked so grim? Or was it the missing dragon? Tuuli's stomach growled at the sight of the palace. They hadn't eaten any of the food they brought along. There hadn't been a good time.

Keirosum landed in the palace courtyard after three other dragons. Tuuli got down and said, "Thank you. What will you do now?"

"I believe I shall go back to our caves one last time, feast and sleep."

"Why one last time?"

"In three days all of us are moving back to our old caves. The ones inside Faerie."

"Why three days?"

"It is an auspicious day for us. Our oldest surviving elder was born on that day. In Faerie. In three days she will return to Faerie, to our beautiful painted caves."

"That will be wonderful," said Tuuli.

"Yes, it will."

Tuuli said, "Sleep well then."

She stood against the palace wall, watching him take off.

Feeling rather alone.

CHAPTER 22 ~ ADAIRE

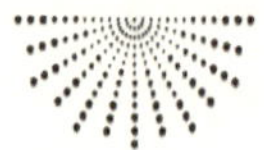

Adaire climbed down the rigging and off of Ethelgarde, making sure to tell him it needed repairing. Skye followed behind, obviously eager to get off the dragon's back. The sylph must have squirmed the entire ride back to Faerie. Adaire had forgotten how much energy Skye exuded. At all times.

Meredith rushed out of the palace to greet Skye and Kian, hugging them. Aura and the other elders followed close behind. Along with the crowd who must be breakfasting at the palace.

Adaire walked to Ethelgarde's head and said, "Thank you so much for your help. It means a lot to get everyone into Faerie, safe."

"You are very welcome. I will go and check on Halvor and Maximus."

"I hope they're going to be all right. If there's anything we can do, please let me know."

"Our healers will be there soon. And here comes three of your healers. I will take them to see if they can help."

"What about the other dragon? I don't even know his name."

"*Her* name is Tavora. She is coming. She is not injured, just badly frightened by the Fomorians She will be all right."

Adaire turned to see Willow, Rush and Teasel climbing up the rigging. Each had a basket of what must be healing supplies.

"I will see you soon," Adaire said.

"I am looking forward to it."

She walked towards the palace, along with everyone else.

Once the healers were strapped in, Ethelgarde lumbered to the pool end of the courtyard and turned his bulky body in the small space. Then he ran, the earth shaking, until he reached the edge of the stairs. He extended his wings and soared off over the stairway. Flapping his wings, the dragon circled until he'd gained enough height to fly over the tree tops.

One by one, the other dragons took off, either flying in the direction to return to their caves, or going to help the two wounded dragons.

Kian, Dylan, Egan and Fiachna stood together, talking animatedly. Fiachna had a bloody gash on his face and another on his arm. He must have been injured by the Fomorians. And she hadn't even noticed it while they flew.

"That was magnificent," said Meredith. "I never tire of watching them come and go."

"I don't understand," said Skye. "How did we become friends with the dragons?"

"It's a very long story," said Meredith.

"Short version," said Skye.

"You sylphs, always in a hurry. Well, they used to be part of Faerie, long ago. Egan asked their help in fighting the Fomorians after Faerie was closed. They agreed to help, if we would teach them our magic. And in a few days, they're moving back into their old caves, which are painted in the most extraordinary fashion. You'll have to go see them."

"Okay, I'll do that. I want to understand how one of our oldest enemies have become our friends."

"Let's get you some breakfast and we'll fill you in on what's been happening since you've been gone," said Meredith.

Adaire didn't want to follow them. She wanted to walk in the woods.

"I'll see you later," she said.

"You should join us," said Meredith.

"Some other time. I'm really tired. I haven't slept in what feels like a very long time."

"All right. But come back to the palace when you wake," said Meredith.

"I will," said Adaire, knowing she wouldn't.

It was warm here by the palace. She suddenly remembered the clothes she'd put on last night for flying.

Adaire peeled off the wool sweater. Then sat on a short stone wall and unlaced the soft leather boots, slipping them off. Removed the deerskin pants.

She left the clothes on the greenstone wall and whispered to the palace, "Thank you."

The palace would see that the clothes were cleaned and returned to wherever they belonged, for the next user.

She watched Tuuli join the crowd moving into the palace. The sylph belonged there, with all the others. Adaire didn't.

A mixture of sadness and warmth flushed through Adaire's body, making her feel awkward and alone.

It was not to be.

Adaire turned away and padded down the stone stairs, across the road and towards the woods. She loosened the braids on her long hair and dropped the leather tie on the earth.

She stepped down the earthen path, the scent of the damp earth surrounded her. The smell of her forests. The cleanliness of fresh soil filled with the abundant roots of happy plants. The dirt between her bare toes felt perfect.

"My friends, I've missed you so." She caressed an ash tree's rough, diamond-like bark. The moist, mossy soil sank beneath her weight.

"Spring has come. Soon, summer will be upon us."

The bluebells had begun to bloom. Their fragrance so strong, she could almost taste their sweetness.

Here, here in the forest were her lovers.

Not up at the palace. She belonged to the woods. No matter how desirable she found Tuuli, the sylph didn't return her feelings. Probably never would.

It was foolish to maintain hope that anything would come of it other than friendship.

Which wasn't enough.

She needed to be in the woods. To reclaim her own life. Her mostly solitary life.

Perhaps, it was time.

Time to do what many dryads did. To join with a tree. Become one with it and live out the rest of her life beneath its comforting bark. Connect her mind with the sensuality of an oak, feeling the pulsing of the seasons.

To let someone else care for the injured parts of the forest.

She felt weary of wounds and death. Of war. Of Fomorians.

Far better to immerse herself in the vital, luminous life of an oak tree.

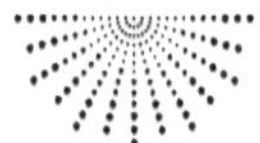

Once inside the palace, Tuuli undressed and left her clothes in the entryway where they seemed to be kept these days.

She thought about going up to her room, to be alone. But her stomach growled with complaint. And she could smell cooked sausage.

Inside the throne room, the tables were full.

Aura caught her eye and said, "Come sit by me."

Tuuli sat on the bench next to the elder.

Skye and Meredith were sitting across from them.

Skye was eating ravenously, as if she'd been starving to death.

Tuuli poured herself a cup of tea. Then she put a sausage and some eggs on a plate. She bit into the sausage, the rich, meaty flavor filled her mouth. She closed her eyes in bliss.

Meredith was telling Skye about how their friendship with the dragons began. Occasionally the sylph paused between mouthfuls to look up, her eyes wide. Especially when Aura spoke about Tuuli's part in rescuing the sylphs.

Finally Skye finished. She pushed her empty plate away.

"Sorry, I'd forgotten about the food in Faerie. It's so extraordinary. I've been famished, eating only human food for so long. Their food tastes so thin and flavorless. It just not nourishing like food from Faerie."

"It's all right," said Meredith. "I fully understand."

Tuuli knew Meredith had also spent millennia in the human world. Skye, Adaire, Dylan and Egan had too. It was such a strange thing. Why would anyone choose to do such a thing?

Skye looked at Tuuli and asked, "How are you recovering from that? Losing your wings?"

Tuuli wanted to squirm, like a child being put on the spot.

How was she recovering?

By not thinking about it. By keeping busy, rescuing others mostly. By flying away on a dragon whenever she could.

"I am doing well," she lied.

"You know, among humans there are women who have gotten a disease and had to have their breasts removed to cut out the disease. It sounds strange to us, with our healing powers. But for humans, breasts are very important. Because sex is very important to them. So for a woman to have her breasts cut off in order to save her life, it is a very brave act. Still, many of them are devastated. They feel less than they are. To reclaim that part of themselves, some get tattoos, beautiful drawings of colored inks drawn on their skin. To make themselves feel whole again. I've seen some of them on women who've come to me for healing. It's quite an extraordinary gesture for them."

Tuuli thought about it, and said, "I think it is different though. Without my wings, it is almost as if I am no longer a sylph. I cannot live with the other sylphs, can not even fly up to the nest anymore. The only way I can fly is on the back of a dragon. And I was used to flying everywhere."

"I'm not saying it's exactly the same. I'm saying that you've lost a huge, important part of yourself. I was just wondering how you were overcoming that loss. Nosy of me, I know," said Skye, her head cocked in a gesture of tenderness.

It was not like sylphs to be secretive. Yet Tuuli didn't want to share her guiltiness at abandoning herself.

She picked up the remaining sausage, stood and said, "I am fine. Just fine, considering what has happened."

Then she walked towards the door.

Behind her, Tuuli heard Skye say, "I didn't mean to insult her."

Aura gave a deep sigh and said, "It had to be done, Skye."

Tuuli went out into the hallway and through the front door of the palace. Feeling incredibly guilty for having been so rude. But also, totally unrepentant.

She headed down the stone steps, across the road and down a path through the woods. Moving generally towards the ancient dragon caves.

It would take her most of the day to walk there. It would have been such a short time to fly. But without wings, that wasn't possible.

The forest was alive with sound. Robins and thrushes sang. Wrens flittered through the bushes. It must have rained recently, everything was damp. The smell of wet soil filled the air.

Hazelnut trees were bare of leaves, but filled with tasseled flowers.

Tuuli kept walking until she was out of the woods and into a grassy meadow. Butterflies, mostly orange, but with four, bluish-white eyes on their wings fluttered among the flowers popping up through the grass.

She held her hand out and one landed on it, using the resting space to clean its antennae. The tiny movements tickled her hand.

It was spring and the world was coming alive again.

But she felt all wrong.

She didn't feel dead, more like she'd eaten too many wild raspberries and nothing else. Jittery. Avoiding the real issue.

Which was, who was she now? Now that she didn't belong with the sylphs, other than being a wingless mascot.

And she didn't want that.

Overhead, a cloud of crows cackled and dove at a hawk, chasing it out of the meadow.

Tuuli plonked down into the deep, wet grass, then she lay on her back. The grass and flowers beneath her, both tickling her skin and cushioning her body.

She watched birds, butterflies and a myriad of insects fly past. Occasionally, a dragon or two flew over, carrying what looked like bundles.

They must have begun the process of moving into their old caves.

She smiled, hoping they would be surprised at the decorated floor that she, Adaire and Dylan had found.

Her leg itched and she raised up onto her elbows to see what it was.

Her entire body was covered with fluttering butterflies, like the orange ones she'd seen earlier as well as some that were white, and others that had small light, greenish-yellow wings. They just sat on her, opening and closing their wings.

She thought about Skye's comment. Maybe she should get a huge set of butterfly wings painted on her back, like those human women. Become a nurturer of butterflies, like Adaire had said.

Tuuli lay back down in the long foliage and watched the high white, gray clouds drift past. She let herself cry out her pain. Over her lost wings, her loneliness and her feelings of belonging nowhere.

Then she fell lost into sleep, still covered in butterflies. Held by the earth.

CHAPTER 24 ~ ADAIRE

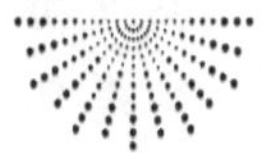

Adaire woke lying on the mossy ground beneath a great oak. How long had she slept? A day? Two?

Not long. The oak was still bare, its leaf buds swelling and getting ready to open.

She stretched her long body and stood.

Walking over to a nearby stream, she scooped up the cold, fresh water and drank it from her hand, until her thirst felt quenched. The water in Faerie tasted better than anywhere in the world. It came from sacred springs deep within the earth.

She rubbed some water over her face and stood looking about her.

The sky colored with salmon and lilac. Dawn. It was dawn. She could hear the trees around her whisper of those who would never awaken again. The trees around the edges of Faerie. Those burned in the battles with the Fomorians.

Adaire knew she should return to her work. Trying to heal those trees which were injured.

She looked in the direction of the palace, hidden from her sight by the yews, pines and hollies.

She wanted to be with Tuuli.

But it probably wasn't the best thing for the sylph. She should be spending time with other sylphs. Maybe now that Skye was back, Skye could help her heal. Skye had lived in the human world long enough, that like Adaire, she needed something to do.

Doing not being. That was a human thing, not Fae. They were more gifted at being. Doing took effort for Fae, and didn't come as naturally.

Adaire walked past the oaks, her hands brushing their bare branches.

Had she been so tainted by humans that she'd lost the ability to go into a tree and just be?

It probably didn't matter right now.

There was much work to be done. Trees and shrubs that needed healing. Spring was here and some of the trees had woken up injured and broken.

There was more to be done than there were dryads to do the work.

Adaire spread out her awareness farther. She could feel where others were working. There. There was a place at the edge of Faerie where the forest was hurting the most.

She headed down a path towards the northern edge of Faerie. Moving over spongy, humusy soil made walking effortless. Breathing the fresh, moist air, she picked up her pace. Touching bare tree branches and those with new spring green leaves alike, Adaire passed through the woods, leaving plants glowing with vitality. This was the dryads' gift.

Occasionally, she plucked a birch or hawthorn leaf and chewed it as she moved along. The birch leaves were sweeter, the hawthorn very bitter, but it woke her body up, giving her more connection with the forest.

A beautiful red fox, a vixen, crossed her path and stood staring, unafraid.

"Hello friend," she said, continuing on.

It followed her, probably curious.

Adair walked for what must have been hours before she came to the damaged forest. The fox followed along.

The trees here were a mixture of ash, beech and hazelnut. Not many evergreens. Large trees were completely burnt on the outside. Dead on the inside.

Her heart sank at the destruction. She left many of the dead ones standing. Tending to the injured instead. Trees that might still be salvaged if she removed dead and dying branches. And given a little extra boost of her healing energy.

The vixen sat perched on a fallen log. Watching her.

Finally exhausted, Adaire sat down on the log.

"Why are you here? Is there something I can do for you?" she asked the fox.

The fox walked across the log to her and sniffed Adaire's hand, cautiously.

Then rubbed up against it.

Adaire petted the creature's coarse fur. It felt soft compared to the tree bark on the log beneath her. The vixen closed her eyes in pleasure. Clearly some human or Fae had spent time with her. Tamed her. Most foxes were wild, even to Fae.

She was young, and since she'd followed Adaire this far, clearly didn't have babies. Most vixens would be in a burrow this time of year, taking care of kits.

"What are you doing out in the world following me?"

She continued to pet the fox, while resting. The vixen studied Adaire with her beautiful golden eyes.

The fox seemed to want nothing more than attention.

Adaire got up and sat cross legged on the mossy ground, leaning her back against the scratchy log.

The fox jumped down beside her, then climbed in Adaire's lap and curled up, wrapping the long, luxuriant tail around her delicate black paws

Adaire smiled and continued petting her.

She was too empty to heal any more trees today. Her magic had been expended. She needed to rest and refill again.

So she sat, soaking up the earth's energy. Feeling the warm fox on her lap. Watching songbirds flit between the budded out branches of trees and shrubs. Elderberry bushes nearly blooming, dog rose buds swelling. Another month of so before they would flower.

The forest was coming back to life. The cycle would begin again. The dead trees would decay, providing food for the seeds that would be born from these flowers. There would be new trees, bushes and other plants. New litters of mice, voles and squirrels would inhabit these woods. Bats would make their homes in the larger burned out trees, as they decayed and formed hollows in the massive trunks.

It would take decades, but this part of Faerie would again become a thriving woodland again. Such was the cycle of life. All she could do was tend this magnificent garden, adding muscle, magic and attention where it was needed.

Adaire stroked the sleeping fox. What was her story? Had she been abandoned by the being who tamed her? Or just wandered off? Did she lack the ability to be with her own kin? To find a mate? Was she an outcast like Adaire?

She sighed, longing for a love that wasn't meant to be.

Adaire was obviously meant to be alone. She'd had one great love. Perhaps, that was all her life would hold.

But she had friends. This vixen. And Ethelgarde.

When Adaire finished here, she should go to the dragon caves and see him.

CHAPTER 25 ~ TUULI

TUULI MADE HER WAY THROUGH THE FOREST, THE mountain looming in front of her. The trees she walked between were bare and small. Little more than seedlings. She had no idea what they were, Adaire would have known.

Their small leaves were barely open, not quite unfurled yet. So they didn't really block her view of the barren mountain. Well, not completely barren. There were a few scrubby looking plants clinging to the rocks, fighting for life.

This whole section of Faerie looked rather desolate and harsh. Even the short trees weren't thriving. How long had the dragons been gone from here? It looked like no time at all.

Perhaps most living things had heard they were returning, picked up their roots and moved.

Living near dragons probably wasn't healthy for much of anything.

Smoke rose up through a hole in the rocks. Quite a lot of it. Were the dragons trying to stay warm? It was quite a lovely spring-like day.

She sent a message with her mind, *"Keirosum?"*

"I can hear you."

"I would like to come visit, can I?"

"Certainly, we would be honored. Where are you?"

"At the foot of the mountain."

"Do you want me to come get you?"

"No, I will climb up. I just wanted know if I was welcome."

"You are most welcome."

Tuuli began to climb up the rough gray stones. There was an ancient trail, but it was a mess from disuse and hard to find in places. She should probably tell one of the stone Fae. They would see that it was cleaned up.

She felt sweaty and out of breath. And dusty from climbing over all the rubble. All the millennia of debris that she, Adaire and Dylan had magicked over the edge had ended up down here. Tuuli was just stirring it all up again.

By the time she reached the top, not only Keirosum, but many other dragons were peering over the edge of the cave opening.

"Well hello," he said. "We were not expecting anyone to come visit so soon. It is enchanting to see you."

"I was wandering and saw some of you moving in. I thought I would come see what all of you thought about the floor."

"There has been much delight surrounding the floor. We have brought water up here to clean it further."

She noticed that despite the many dragons walking all over it, the floor gleamed in the sunlight. It looked even more beautiful than when she'd seen it last.

The fire pits were empty and cleaned out. There wasn't even any ashes in them.

"Where is the smoke coming from?"

"The caves where our eggs are waiting to hatch. Would you like to see them?"

"Yes."

She had a feeling that this was a great honor.

Keirosum led her across the main cave with the painted floor. There must have been seventy dragons there, but it looked spacious. Some were sprawled out, sleeping in the sun.

A couple of groups of dragons were gathered around a spread-out hide and worked with powders and pools of colored liquid, mixing them together with either a long claw or with sticks. Others looked as if they were repainting the walls of the open cave.

One held a stick, the end of which had been wrapped with bits of animal fur. Tuuli had never really noticed that the dragons actually had long, slender fingers with claws at the tips. The dragon had wrapped its fingers around the stick and used the claw to tip the brush ever so slightly, making paint flow from the animal fur. It dipped the end back into some paint and made another line, this one became the curve of a dragon's back and the tail. Tuuli could see that the dragon copied the faded original, line for line. It was remarkably detailed.

"There is much restoration to do," said Keirosum. "The oldest paintings are fading. We must repaint them before they disappear."

Tuuli followed him down a wide tunnel that had smaller caves opening from it, like rooms in the palace. These rooms were jammed full of sleeping dragons, curled around each other like sleeping baby squirrels. The dragons looked smaller than Keirosum, who as a male was smaller than the females. Perhaps, they were young ones.

Far into the mountain, at the end of the tunnel was another

cave. She could feel the warmth before she entered it. There were two adult dragons, adding wood to a fire and stirring it. Another adult moved carefully among the eggs, which were as tall as Tuuli's shoulder, turning them. The eggs were different colors, shades of green, blue, black and purple. They glittered in the dim light of the fire.

The heat made Tuuli sweat even more.

Most of the smoke escaped out through a hole in the ceiling. It must be a very long tunnel to the outside. But a great deal of the smoke stayed in the cave and made it hard for Tuuli to breathe. The smell was overwhelming, and with every breath she wanted to cough. But out of politeness, she suppressed it.

"This is one of our egg caves. There is another through there. For the ruby, golden, amber and carnelian colored eggs."

"You separate your eggs according to color?"

"Those colors need more heat, both in the eggs, and in the hatchlings. The adults too, for that matter, appreciate warmth more. Blue and green dragons often swim, and even enjoy coolness."

"I had no idea. Then flying to rescue the sylphs must have been torture for you."

"No, we enjoy the heat, that does not mean we can not tolerate the cold. It is simply not enjoyable."

Tuuli realized that there were no paintings on the walls, which were black. When she asked about this, Keirosum explained.

"It is the smoke, you see. It colors the walls. Any paintings would be completely lost. But the floor is decorated."

She looked down and saw intricate designs on the floor. Stones and pieces of shells were inlaid in the floor.

"This is beautiful."

"The young have poor eyesight at first. So we give them beauty nearby to look at and touch."

The three adult dragons rushed over to one of the eggs, which was rocking. They stood around it, waiting.

Keirosum said, "Your arrival is auspicious. This will be the first hatching that has happened here in millennia."

Tuuli's eyes widened.

The green egg began to crack, long streaks appearing down the sides. Then the tip of a clubbed tail broke through the top. The egg split open as if someone had put all four limbs on each side and pushed out on all equally.

In the middle of the pile of egg shells stood a slimy green and blue dragon. Its eyes were amber colored and looked unfocused. It had fleshy protrusions that looked like drooping spikes around its neck, down the back and on the end of the club tail.

Keirosum said, "Oh, she is lovely. The spikes on her neck and back will stand up as she ages."

The baby dragon gave out a squealing sound that filled the room. Then she proceeded to eat some of the egg shell.

Tuuli just stared in wonder at the cow-sized creature. It looked so vibrant and full of life.

"The shell contains the perfect first food for baby dragons. Once it is done eating, it will sleep again. Then wake, eat and sleep. That is the way of the young. In the meantime, most of the others will hatch out."

"Most, but not all?" Tuuli asked.

"There are always one or two who hatch much later. After all the other young have moved out of the hatching cave. Perhaps those eggs were laid later, perhaps they need more time with the heat. It is always the way."

The baby dragon stopped eating and began walking

clumsily on the decorative floor. It frequently ran into something, often one of the adult dragons. When it ran into one of them, it sat down on its haunches and studied the dragon or egg. Now and then it squealed softly, as if first discovering its voice.

Tuuli had never been around young. There weren't many young Fae and their mothers often kept them secluded. At least air Fae did. Until the young's wings were developed enough so that they could fly. The sylphs homes were high up in the cliffs and falling off them was a danger to the precious few young.

Watching the baby dragon fascinated her.

Rarely had she seen anything this young. Although once she happened upon a linnet nest and watched the eggs hatch. Tuuli saw it from a distance as she hadn't wanted to frighten the mother bird away. But it had been wondrous.

This felt no different. What an amazing creature the dragon was.

The baby dragon wandered her way and suddenly began to move quickly towards her. Keirosum stopped it from running into her, by putting his tail against the baby's shoulders.

The baby dragon squealed in surprise.

"She is very strong," he said.

"Can I touch her?" Tuuli asked.

"Certainly," he said.

Tuuli reached out and stroked the dragon's shoulder. The baby came up to her waist when standing. It watched her hand and when she touched it, the baby's eyes closed and it let out a deep sigh.

"You have made her very happy," said Keirosum.

The baby dragon curled up in a ball, almost cooing and began to sleep.

Then she noticed other eggs cracking and the adult dragons paying attention to them.

"We should leave," said Keirosum. "If they run into you, they might injure you. They have no control over their actions."

"Of course," she said.

As she moved out of the cave, two more babies were emerging from their shells. One of the adults had placed its thick tail across the cave entrance to make sure no one escaped.

"Is it usual to have so many eggs in a season?"

"No. There are two reasons for this. One is the joy and renewal we dragons have felt at the anticipated return to Faerie. The other is the loss of so many of us to the Fomorians. And the knowledge that this war is far from over."

Tuuli sighed deeply.

The war. It was easy to forget the war with everyone safe inside Faerie.

What was the Council going to do next?

CHAPTER 26 ~ ADAIRE

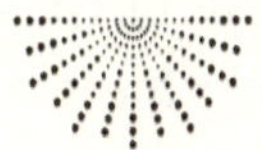

ADAIRE MOVED THROUGH THE OPEN MEADOW. THE lake was alive with water Fae. Spring was definitely here.

They were rollicking, three or four young sprites, chasing each other across the surface of the lake. She smiled at their antics.

The vixen sat at her feet, watching them with fascination.

The fox had been following her for three days and nights now. Adaire had taken to calling her Rowan. The fox's red-orange fur reminded her of rowan berries.

Adaire had spent two days working at healing the damaged forest which bordered the burnt out section. Having done what she could, now it was time to let them grow on their own for a while. She headed towards the dragons' painted caves.

She nibbled on some sweet birch leaves, from trees that grew near a stream which fed the lake. Then thanked the trees for their bounty.

Then waded through the cold stream, using the water to wash herself. As Adaire washed her face and long hair, she sipped some of the fresh water. It tasted like soil, there were a lot of minerals in the water of Faerie.

When she finished, Adaire stepped out on the far bank. The fox waded through the water, swimming when it got too deep. Once out of the stream, the vixen shook, then bathed herself. Licking her fur like a cat. Finally, she hurried after Adaire.

They moved through the birches on the other side of the stream and then into another meadow.

Adaire felt tired. She hadn't traveled like this, stopping to heal trees as she went, for a very long time.

The sun came out from behind the clouds; the grass and wildflowers were new and fresh. Fat bumblebees buzzed between plump blossoms. Faerie was abundant.

She sat down in the tall grass and flowers, smelling the scent of the sweet pale yellow pansies which surrounded her. Rowan plopped down nearby and continued drying herself.

Adaire decided she had traveled far enough for the time being.

She searched for insects, trying not to crush anyone, then lay back in the soft meadow grass. After a time Rowan stretched out beside her, the fox's nose twitching as she took in every smell that came in on the changing breeze.

Adaire loved the feel of the warm sun on her skin. It had been a long, difficult winter. The spring sun felt so welcome.

Far above, a large raptor circled. Perhaps looking for a mouse or hare meal in the meadow below. Perhaps annoyed at Adaire's presence.

She sent her energy deep into the soil, feeling the nearby plants' roots and those of the closest trees. A large oak and a cluster of beeches. Here in the heart of Faerie at least, the trees were happy. Contented. They didn't share the pain and grief of those damaged at the edges of Faerie.

It made her feel at ease. It was difficult to spend all of one's time around so much pain. Adaire had known this when she was younger. But it seemed she needed to relearn it.

When next the dryads met, she would bring this up. That the healers needed to heal as well.

So she basked in the sunlight, in the trees' contentment, and in the vixen's presence. Soaking it all up, filling up on the gifts of Faerie.

By mid-afternoon, the sun left the meadow.

Adaire got up and continued walking towards the mountain which held the dragon caves. Rowan followed her.

Adaire spent a great deal of the time rethinking what she should do about her feelings for Tuuli. She came to no conclusions, only growing more confused.

The mountain loomed in front of her by the time the sun moved below the trees. She curled up next to a large pine trunk, Rowan next to her for companionship, Adaire guessed.

The next morning Adaire woke before the sun, listening to the finches sing in the day. The smell of resin from decades of dropped pine needles filled her nose. She stood, stretching. Her muscles no longer felt sore from days of walking.

Rowan had gone during the night sometime, and must have heard Adaire waking. The vixen returned with a tiny dead mouse. She sat and delicately ate it.

When she'd finished, Adaire said, "I'm going to climb up that mountain and go visit the dragons. If you're afraid of dragons, you should stay here, my friend. I'll come back and find you."

Then she found an ancient path up the side of the mountain. Rowan followed her. There was much debris blocking it. Boulders and even small downed trees at the base. It was rough going a lot of the time.

Adaire stopped at a pine that had fallen across the path. She held out her hands, moving energy out the tips of her fingers to cut the pine into pieces and then Piled them beside the path. There they would provide homes for insects as the wood decayed and returned to nature.

Overhead there was a thundering of wings as three amethyst colored dragons took off, heading over the forest. They hadn't seen her.

Perhaps she should tell Ethelgarde she was here.

'Ethelgarde, I'm here.'

'Where?'

'At the base of your mountain.'

'Are you coming up?'

'Yes, is that all right?'

'You are most welcome here.'

Rowan was still watching the dragons, her ears twitched warily.

"It's all right dear. If you want to go wait for me in the woods, I'll understand."

The fox twitched her ears again, looked concerned, yet she followed Adaire up the mountain.

At one blocked place on the path, a grayish brown lizard sat on a rock, basking in the sun. It quickly disappeared as Adaire came closer.

She moved the stones, what humans would call two-man rocks, lifting and placing them at the side of the path. Stone Fae would have known the right request to make, to have the rocks move themselves, but she'd never studied stone lore. Perhaps she should.

Adaire kept climbing, following the path as it switched back and forth across the face of the mountain. Above her, she could see the open side of the cave. There were several dragons watching her progress.

The sun rose higher in the sky and the side of the mountain grew warmer. The rocks soaked up the heat and held it. Probably it was warm up here even at night.

After midday, she finally made it to the cave.

By now there were at least twenty dragons waiting for her.

"Hello," she said. "I brought a friend with me. Is she safe here?"

Ethelgarde said, "We do not hunt foxes. Yes, she is safe."

Adaire reached down and patted Rowan, who was pressed against her leg. She must have understood, because the vixen sat down and stared at the dragons with alert eyes, her nose twitching.

Adaire recognized several of the dragons, Attania, Goshania, Marusa, Iru, Spike, Carbon and Silver.

She bowed at them and they bowed their heads in response.

"How are you enjoying being back in your old caves?"

Silver, an elder with sparkly, silver scales said, "We have felt at home the instant we returned. I was so young when we left, I almost did not remember the beautiful painted floor in this open area. Spike said that you are one of the Fae we have to thank for that. Thank you for clearing it for us."

"You're welcome. It was an honor to find it. Your paintings are truly beautiful."

They were interrupted by a squealing sound and a flash of yellow scales.

Instantly three dragons penned the flash in with their tails. Which was followed by more squealing. Then Adaire saw that the yellow thing was a baby dragon. It looked wet and slimy. The wings were small and gooey looking. Its blue eyes appeared unfocused. It sat on its hind legs, staring at her.

She could smell a fishy scent coming from it.

She heard the rumbling of loud, fleshy footsteps and a red dragon came from the same passageway as the baby.

"My apologies. He escaped us."

"Do you need more help?" asked Iru.

"Yes, too many are hatching at once. We need a little help. And we need to get this one back inside before he gets too cold."

"I will help, then," he said.

With their tails, they herded the baby back inside the hallway.

Adaire realized she'd been standing there with her mouth open. She had not expected to see a baby dragon. It hadn't even entered her mind that they existed.

"We are going to have a lot of hatchlings this season," said Silver. "It has been a very long time. Our numbers have been dwindling ever since Faerie was closed, and us on the outside of it. As soon as your elders gave us permission to return to Faerie, our joy allowed many of us to become fertile again."

"We are excited at all the youngsters who have been hatched," said Attania, a sapphire colored dragon.

"Even our elders who had faded and grown unresponsive have come back to us. This is such a relief. We have long been afraid of losing our wisdom," said Goshania, whose scales were like emeralds.

Ethelgarde said, "It is true. We are being revived."

He opened his wings, stretching and fluttering them slightly.

His ivory scales flashed in the sunlight, revealing an opalescent show of colors. Red, greens, blues and yellows shone out, changing with every movement. He was quite the most beautiful dragon she had ever seen.

"I am happy to hear of your good fortune."

"Will you tell the others?" asked Silver. "Thank your elders for us?"

"I will," said Adaire. "Although I might not be back to the palace for some time. I'm wandering the forests, healing the trees. Isn't Dylan a better choice for your messenger?"

The other dragons looked at Spike. He was a big black dragon with fleshy spikes around his neck, like a collar. His head hung down, and he reminded Adaire of a dejected dog.

"Dylan has not called me for a long time. The water folk are waking and he is their leader now."

"Why isn't Meredith their leader?" A feeling of dread filled her.

"She is on the council now. She cannot be at the lake as well. At least that is what Dylan told me. He has to be down at the lake, teaching those whose powers are less than his. Helping them grow. I do not understand it. He should be painting."

"He is very skilled," said Ethelgarde.

"He's also the most powerful water Fae after Meredith," said Adaire. "He needs to pass his knowledge on. I understand. But he also needs to paint. And I'm guessing Solange misses him too."

"I believe she does," said Spike. "But I cannot speak to her mind. Humans have not developed that ability. Although I do like her and she likes me."

"I'll return to the palace then," said Adaire. "Give the elders your message, and then I'll go find Dylan and speak with him."

"Would you like a ride?" asked Ethelgarde.

"I would, but there are trees I must speak with, and I don't think my friend Rowan here is quite trusting enough to fly with you," she said. "I will return, alone next time, and accept your offer of a ride somewhere. I miss flying with you."

He bowed his head at her. Rowan walked towards the dragon's nose, licked it and then returned to Adaire.

Ethelgarde made a rasping, chuckling sound.

Adaire bowed at all the dragons.

Carbon had been over at one of the fire pits. He returned, holding something in his claws.

"Here is some roasted deer we cooked this morning. You look hungry."

Adaire realized she was. She took the small chunk of charred meat and said, "Thank you. I am hungry."

She pulled some off and began to chew it. It was smokey and crispy on the surface, but tender and juicy beneath. Perfectly cooked.

"How did you cook it?" she asked.

Carbon said, "We stack up the firewood, put the meat on it, then one of us flames the wood. Someone will turn the meat. That's about it."

She offered some to Rowan, but the fox showed no interest. Most wild creatures didn't like cooked meat.

It took less than half the time to get down the mountain, as to get up. At least she didn't have to stop and clear the trail.

Still it was dusk by the time she made it to the forest floor. White moths had come out and were fluttering through the mist.

It was the in-between time. When she loved Faerie most. The trees formed dim silhouettes shooting up from the ground and the fog tangled between them. She could feel the dampness on her skin. The pine needles crunched beneath her feet, damp on the outside from all the rain. But still crispy on the inside.

Rowan followed her, circling around her legs when Adaire stopped. The vixen's coarse fur felt soft against her skin.

Adaire caught a scent, which made her heart beat faster. She followed it through the darkness. There, where the forest ringed a meadow, on the far edge stood a tree in full bloom. White blossoms weighed down the branches.

The first hawthorne of the season. The signal that summer was here. Beltaine. May Day as the humans called it.

Every year it was a different tree in another part of Faerie. The land always changed. Nothing stayed the same within Faerie.

She needed to report the sighting to the palace. To be a dryad who found the first hawthorne blossoms of Beltaine didn't happen often. Usually it was the sylphs who got that honor. There were so much faster.

"You ready to run, dear girl?"

The vixen yipped at her.

Adaire began to run. Jumping over logs, racing down deer trails.

The fox fast at her heels.

CHAPTER 27 ~ TUULI

AFTER TUULI LEFT THE DRAGONS, SHE WANDERED through the forest for a day, speaking with dragonflies, butterflies, bees, and any insect who would take the time to stop and talk with her.

It was evening and she sat on a soft mossy log, a white moth on her hand. The moon shone through an opening in the tree canopy above, pooling around her like a sumptuous cloak. The moth told her of the lovely nectar to be found in nearby blooming trees. But also its fear of bats. A large brown bat nearly caught the moth just last night.

The night was perfumed with the white blossoms of blackthorn trees. Which was why Tuuli had paused here in the first place. This clearing was one of the things she loved best about Faerie.

The moon, the white flowers, the moth sitting on her hand, others fluttering through the night. The scent of the flowers, the moist dewy air surrounding her.

Magic flowed through the moonlight like kestrels floating on an updraft. Everything around her spoke of rebirth. The land coming alive for summer. The bare trees had either covered themselves in leaves, or would soon. Bluebells clothed the forest floor, their sweet scent mingling with that of the blackthorn. Purple flowers setting off all the new chartreuse tree leaves.

The forest was gaudy at this time of year. A riot of color and sensation.

Insects, birds, hares, martins and badgers were all waking from the cold winter. Ready to have their young.

The moth fluttered away to sip more nectar.

Tuuli breathed deeply, taking in all that Faerie had to offer.

She could do this.

Wander the forests. Help the winged insects and those birds who lived near the ground. After the last day of walking and communicating with them, it was clear to her. They had been ignored by the sylphs. They too could use healing. Especially the bees.

Tuuli stood and began walking through the moonlight. She loved the way the forest looked at night. The blossoming trees glowed. Shimmering water of the streams. The way the softness of the moss felt even gentler on her feet. The rasping barks of foxes fighting over territory. The taste of all the strongly perfumed flowers on her tongue.

By the time Tuuli reached the palace, her stomach rumbled. It was still dark outside, the moon was on its way to setting.

She walked across the cool stones in the entry way. The throne room was dark and almost empty, still sleeping. There was a fire Fae keeping a blaze in a fire pit going. A sylph, probably having imbibed too much wine to safely fly home, slept curled up on one of the wood benches near the fire.

Tuuli walked through the room and towards the kitchens.

Light spilled out into the darkened hallway. The smooth stone floor felt warm from the ovens.

In the kitchen four earth Fae were busy cooking. One chopped potatoes. A green skinned earth spirit flattened dough of some sort. A rather tall Fae stirred a pot on the wood stove. The last was crumbling herbs over a bowl.

Tuuli could smell the yeast of rising dough and bacon and onions frying.

"Oh, you are up early," said the earth spirit who was crumbling herbs.

"I have been walking all night," she said.

"Well, then you will be looking for something to eat. We have some hot water on the stove. I will make some tea. And there are last night's biscuits in that basket. How about if I put some bacon, mushrooms and onions over them?"

"That sounds delicious," said Tuuli, her mouth watering from all the delicious smells.

She watched as the short, copper skinned Fae put tea leaves in a pot and poured in hot water. Then she split a biscuit and put it on a brown stoneware plate, setting the plate on the stove and scooping dripping bacon and onions from a frying pan.

"There is a sauce on it, so give it a minute to soak into the biscuit and soften them up a bit," she said, handing Tuuli the plate.

"Thank you."

"I will bring you your tea in two minutes."

"I'll go sit at a table, then," Tuuli said, understanding she'd been dismissed.

She returned to the throne room. The palace had begun to light candles, so there was a dim glow to the room, perfect for early, early morning.

Putting her plate down on a table, she sat on a hard wooden bench. The food tasted lovely. The bacon, mushrooms and onions mingled perfectly with the biscuit. By the time the kitchen Fae brought her tea, she'd cleaned her plate.

"You were hungry. In just a few minutes there will be some fresh scones out of the oven."

"Lovely," said Tuuli. "It was delicious."

"Thank you," said the cook. "The food will be even better once we put some eggs with it."

A fire Fae blew fire onto a piece of wood and set it to flaming then laid it in the fire pit nearest the front of the room. He tended the fire there and Tuuli could feel the warmth after a short time. She nodded a thanks to him.

Wrapping her hands around her warm cup, she picked the tea up and carried it over to sit on a wooden chair by the fire.

The tea was black with lavender in it. She sipped the strong liquid, feeling the heat move through her body. Out in the woods Tuuli hadn't even realized she was cold. Sylphs grew used to the cold. Sometimes they wore clothes, but mostly fabric just added extra weight and slowed them down. Walking was so different than flying.

But she saw and felt so much more when she walked. She'd never really considered the lives of insects before. And yet, they were as important a part of Faerie as sylphs.

The kitchen Fae put out the scones, teapots, cream and butter. Several other palace Fae came and put plates, cups and silverware on the tables. Soon, other Fae began to filter into the room.

Tuuli stayed near the fire, sipping her tea.

Through the windows she could see dawn crossing the sky in colors of flaming salmon, purple and a bright pink color. Then the colors faded to a mostly clear, blue sky.

Aura and Meredith came into the room and everyone looked up, Tuuli included. Unconsciously, she could feel their intense power. They were speaking quietly to each other, deep in conversation. They went to an empty table, sitting beside each other and Meredith poured tea for both of them. They continued their conversation as they ate.

Tuuli couldn't tell what they were discussing, but it seemed important. And serious. And they both felt passionate about it.

Solange walked in the room, looked around and spotted Tuuli. She waved and poured herself a cup of tea, then came and sat down near her.

"Good morning," Solange said.

"Good morning."

"How are you? I haven't seen you in quite a while."

"I am feeling well. I have been wandering the woods and fields. Enjoying spring and Faerie," said Tuuli. "And you?"

"Dylan's at the lake. I've been helping Meredith and Aura with their research. But I'm lonely. I'm used to spending as much time as possible in solitude. But I miss Dylan."

"I am sorry. I can keep you company. And Adaire will, I am sure, when she is here. Perhaps you would like to wander with one of us."

Solange stared at her.

"I hadn't thought of that. I'd need to bring food and water. And something to keep me warm at night. But I think I'd like to try that."

"The nights are still quite cool out. Perhaps closer to the Solstice would work better. And there will be berries everywhere by then. Not enough to sustain you probably, but they would provide a bit of food," said Tuuli.

"I haven't seen Adaire. Have you?"

"No, our paths have not crossed."

Tuuli felt uneasy about that. She really liked Adaire, even though the dryad held so much back. But then so had Tuuli. She'd been so unable to face the loss of her wings. And her life as she'd always seen it. But now, she had chosen a new life. Perhaps even one that Adaire could share.

If she so chose.

A group of sylphs came through an upper vent in the side of the palace. There looked to be three such vents in the throne room now. They were essentially holes in the wall, covered with tapestries that could be pulled aside. There was a landing platform on both sides of the hole.

Tuuli watched as the five sylphs stepped off the platform, one at a time, floated down and landed on the floor of the throne room. Skye was one of them, her long white hair streaming behind her, power radiating off her like heat waves from a fire.

The sylph came over to Tuuli and Solange and plopped down a a bench, folding her wings behind her.

"You look well," she said.

"I feel well," said Tuuli.

"Good. I'm happy to hear that. Have you seen Adaire?"

"She hasn't," said Solange. "I just asked her."

"I'm worried," said Skye. "Someone should go look for her. It's not like her to just take off like that. Not without telling her elder at least."

"I can go look for her," said Tuuli. "But I need to speak with Aura first. And she seems too…involved, at the moment."

Solange and Skye looked over at Meredith and Aura. They were still leaned together, speaking quietly. The benches around them conspicuously empty.

"What *are* they talking about?" asked Skye.

"No idea," said Tuuli. "But it looks important."

Then Conley, the fire elder came in to the room, followed by Bryan and Ogden, earth elders. The three sat down across from Aura and Meredith and joined their conversation.

Tuuli watched as Ogden sat back, a look of surprise flashed across his face.

Skye said, "Why don't you go over and ask to speak to Aura? See what they're talking about."

Tuuli looked at the audacious sylph.

"I do not think so."

Still, she felt overwhelmed with curiosity, and dread.

CHAPTER 28 ~ ADAIRE

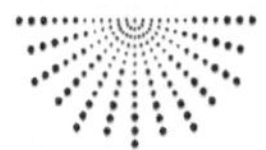

ADAIRE RAN DOWN THE DEER PATH, ARMS HELD OUT in front. Her energy streamed out to move branches and prevent herself from getting slapped in the face by tree branches.

The forest was alive with the scent of pine resin. Red squirrels chattered at her, wondering why she was in such a hurry.

As she ran, her stomach growled. She needed to eat some substantial food. Tree leaves could only sustain a dryad for so long, tasty as they were. She'd get some good food at the palace. Perhaps a meaty pastry. Her mouth watered just thinking of it.

Rowan ran at her heels mostly, content to let Adaire run headfirst into danger.

Adaire slowed after a time. The deer trail ended in a clearing. She bent over, trying to catch her breath. She was in better shape than she had been, but still not at her peak.

Would she ever be again?

Had she passed that time when Fae could no longer regain their youth?

The vixen plopped down in the long grass, panting as well.

Adaire's mouth felt dry. She bent down and picked up a pebble, dusted it off and put it in her mouth to suck on. It tasted earthy from the soil still stuck to it, the flavor was well-balanced and complete. The soil needed no amending.

The meadow was alive with wildflowers: yellow cowslips and dandelions, white fleabane, blue forget-me-nots and purple honesty. There were dozens of different kinds of flowers in bloom. Every bee and butterfly in Faerie was in flight. Collecting or sipping pollen. The fragrance was sweet and heady.

Adaire would have loved to linger. Lie down in the long grass and just be one with the plants.

But she had news to spread and the branch of blossoms to bring.

When her breathing returned to normal, she glanced at the fox. Rowan was also breathing normally.

"You can stay here if you'd like. I need to keep running."

Then she ran for another half a day, faster than any human would have, followed by the vixen. Through pine forests, oak groves and stands of birch. When dusk came, she stopped at a stream. Filling her mouth with the cool clean water, Adaire immersed herself.

The heat of her skin subsided as she bathed. The fox drank daintily from the edge of the stream.

Adaire got out of the water and shook herself dry.

She nibbled on some nearby birch leaves, enjoying their sweetness.

Rowan disappeared into the bushes, probably off to hunt for some dinner.

Adaire sat on the roots of one of the larger birches and fell quickly asleep, listening to the hypnotic churring of a couple of nightjars feeding nearby. She never saw the birds, only heard them. Hoping they weren't included in the fox's dinner plans.

She woke the next morning with the sun rising in the clear sky. It was another chilly morning, with the promise of warmth as the sun rose higher.

Adaire stretched, moving her still aching muscles slowly.

Rowan slept nearby, curled up on a fern. She opened one eye, as if to ask if it was morning already. But the fox didn't move other than that.

She walked back towards the stream and drank deeply. Tonight, she should make it to the palace. Perhaps be the first to have seen a blooming Hawthorne this season.

"I'm going," she said, to Rowan.

As Adaire began to make her way through the birches, she turned back to look. Rowan stood and stretched. She went to the creek and sipped water. Then trotted after Adaire.

"I'm glad of your company, my friend."

They moved into a run.

She stopped to rest near another stream when the sun was at her peak. The woods here were more familiar. They were getting close to the palace.

The nearby trees were oaks. Beneath them spread a footing of sweet woodruff, the tiny white flowers were the distinguishing feature of May wine. Which made Fae quite silly.

Here and there, in clumps as high as her knees grew coralroot with its lavender colored blossoms. The beautiful scene made her feel quite heady.

Adaire heard a large movement in the bushes coming up on

the trail. Over a rise, she saw another Fae walking. Rowan fled and hid behind a log.

How could it be the fox was unafraid of dragons, but hid from unknown Fae?

Adaire stood, waiting. Finally, the Fae moved past the nearby shrubs so that Adaire could see her. Tuuli.

"Well, hello," said Adaire.

"Hello. I have been looking for you."

Tuuli moved close enough to embrace Adaire.

Which puzzled her. Had Tuuli ever hugged her before?

"Why are you looking for me?" Adaire asked.

"Skye is worried about you. She said it was not like you to disappear without a word."

"I'm on my way back to the palace. Is that where she is?"

"Yes. I also wanted to say thank you for the idea about taking care of the low flying creatures. I have been spending a great deal of time walking the woods and meadows and have felt them calling to me. That is what I have chosen to do."

Adaire studied Tuuli.

"I'm glad my advice had some value."

"My only problem with doing this is that as much as I value the company of birds, butterflies and other insects, I need to be around other Fae as well. I guess what I am asking is, would you mind if I traveled with you?"

"Traveled with me?"

Adaire wasn't clear what Tuuli was asking.

"I could walk with you and while you were healing trees in an area, I could tend to the flying creatures. Then when we were both finished, we could move on."

"So, as friends?" asked Adaire.

"Yes, as friends. Although, you must know that I am in love with you. How could anyone who knows you not be?"

Adaire let out a deep breath she hadn't known her body was holding. It felt like someone had knocked the wind out of her.

"I had no idea."

"I know," said Tuuli. "It is not as if I ever said anything. I have been so wrapped up with feeling sorry for myself. I know I am not as old as you, not even close to being as powerful. But I am strong. And I feel things as deeply as you do."

Adaire said nothing. She felt paralyzed.

A strange look crossed Tuuli's face.

She said, "You are not interested. You are just listening to me to be polite. I am sorry."

Adaire said, "No. Don't be sorry. I feel the same way about you, as you do for me. I have since I first met you. I just, … I'm a dryad." She shrugged. "We move so much more slowly than you sylphs. We even think slower. We act slower."

Tuuli smiled at Adaire and touched her arm.

"So, you are saying you love me too?"

"Yes."

"Well then, we will take things slowly. I think our lives will work out perfectly."

"I think you're right," said Adaire.

"Come, I'll walk you back to the crossroads. I'm supposed to go to the lake and talk to Dylan."

"Come with me to the palace. I found a blooming Hawthorn. That news will bring Dylan, and everyone."

"The first Hawthorn of spring," said Tuuli, smiling. "Oh, who's this?"

Adaire followed Tuuli's gaze behind her. Rowan sat a bit behind Adaire, listening to their conversation.

Tuuli squatted down, and Rowan came to her. Tuuli petted the fox.

"This is Rowan. She's been following me for days."

"You are so beautiful," said Tuuli, to the fox.

"Are you sure you want to follow me to the palace? There will be many Fae there," Adaire said, to Rowan.

The fox yipped in reply.

"Okay, let's run then," said Adaire.

And they did. For the rest of the afternoon. Adaire's feet were light. The rest of her felt giddy with joy.

Tuuli loved her.

With that she could deal with anything else that came her way.

CHAPTER 29 ~ TUULI

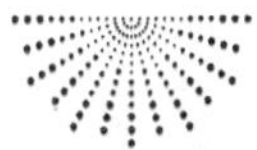

THEY MADE IT TO THE PALACE AS THE SUN WAS
lowering itself below the tree line. It would set in a while, but
the sky hadn't colored up yet.

They washed off in the cold fountains out behind the
palace. The pools were sunk into the earth, lined with smooth
stones and mortar so tight that they held water. Water flowed
out of an ancient sculpture of a nymph's hand, cascading down
her body and back into the pool. The minerals from the water
had added streaks of white to the gray stone. The nymph was
also decorated with lovely green moss.

Even the fox swam a bit before getting out, shaking herself
dry and grooming her fur. Tuuli couldn't understand why the
fox was so eager to follow Adaire to the palace. Was it just
because she didn't want to be parted from Adaire? Or did she
need to come to the palace for some other reason?

Still, Tuuli felt over the moon. Adaire returned her feelings.
Nothing could be better than that.

They shook themselves as dry as possible, but their hair
still dripped as they walked naked into the palace. Her hair was

only down to her shoulders, so had much less to drip than Adaire's knee-length mane.

The throne room was half-full this evening. It was nearly dark inside, not much light was coming through the windows. Dinner was just beginning and it smelled delicious. The scent of roasted meat wafted to her nose. Tuuli's stomach growled with hunger.

There were a couple of fires blazing, even though it felt warm to her. The fire Fae needed the heat.

As they moved through the room, it suddenly lit up with candles and flax seed oil lamps. Everyone looked up as if to wonder who brought the abrupt change in light.

Adaire led the way. She went to the table where the elders ate and leaned down, speaking quietly to Ogden.

He smiled and stood.

"Adaire has an announcement to make," he said, his voice booming through the hall.

Adaire stood back up and held the hawthorne blossoms high above her head.

She said, loud enough for the entire room to hear, "I have found the first blooming hawthorn of summer. Summer is begun!"

Shouts of "Summer is begun!" echoed throughout the room.

Tuuli stood close enough to Adaire that she could feel Rowan sitting at the dryad's feet.

The kitchen Fae brought out May wine and cups to each table. People began pouring it.

Aura made a toast to summer, and they all drank.

The strong taste of the sweet woodruff was balanced by the honey used to sweeten the wine. The wine made Tuuli relax and she sipped it slowly so as not to drink the entire cup until there was some food in her belly.

Adaire motioned to her, and Tuuli followed to an empty bench.

It was then, she noticed that Rowan wasn't following.

The fox went over to Brian, the Earth elder, and pawed at his leg.

He turned, and looked down at the fox, his eyebrows wrinkled in puzzlement.

Tuuli nudged Adaire and pointed.

The fox yipped at Brian. He turned his full attention to the vixen, and then a look of shock crossed his face. Followed by anger.

Those near them turned their attention to what was happening.

Brian lifted the fox in his arms and stood. He left the dining room with her, speaking to no one.

Tuuli looked at Adaire.

"I have no idea. She's been following me for days. Obviously, she had something to say to Brian. Hopefully, we'll find out what. But I need to eat. And I've not been invited to follow."

Tuuli joined her in dishing up some of the roast deer. There was a rich gravy over it that she mopped up with crusty bread. And some lightly cooked greens and onions. Tuuli ate more than she should have, it tasted so good. When she stopped, her belly felt like it would burst.

Skye and Solange came into the throne room and took seats across from them.

"Well, hi stranger," said Skye to Adaire.

"How are you?" asked Adaire.

"I'm doing well. I miss Glastonbury and my clients. I hope

the war ends soon. I'd really like to get back to integrating the human community and opening them up to Faerie."

Adaire sighed.

"I'm not sure how much progress has been made on defeating the Fomorians."

Skye said, "Haven't you heard? Aura and Meredith think they've found a way to, well, not exactly defeat them, but at least come to terms with them."

"We've heard that before," said Adaire.

"Why are you being so negative?" asked Skye.

"I'm tired of this war. I don't even want to think about it anymore. It's awful. The damage its done. I really want it to end. The land isn't benefitting from Faerie being closed, other than the trees aren't getting burned from Fomorians. But Faerie appreciated being open for those few short months. It was like being able to breathe fresh air. The land longs for more of it."

"So, shouldn't you be looking forward to the possibility of a solution?" asked Skye.

Tuuli watched the two of them talk, feeling slightly jealous of Skye's easiness with Adaire. They'd been through a lot together.

"I am looking forward to it," said Adaire. "I'm not looking forward to another let down. So many failures have almost made me lose hope. So I've tried to stay out of it."

Skye shook her head.

Just then Meredith and Aura got up and left the room in a hurry. As if called.

Heads turned.

"I forgot to tell them about the dragons," said Adaire.

"What about the dragons?" asked Solange.

"Their eggs are hatching," said Adaire.

Tuuli stared at Adaire. How did she find out? Perhaps she'd spoken to Ethelgarde.

Tuuli smiled at the thought of the hatchling she'd seen.

"Oh, Dylan will want to know this," said Solange, getting up.

Skye put a hand on her arm.

"Save yourself a trip. Someone will have already run to the lake telling them that summer is here. They'll all be on their way up here. To celebrate," said Skye.

"Someone does need to tell Dylan that Spike misses him terribly. And that he needs to choose another elder to teach the water folk. He needs to be painting and spending some time with his friend, Spike. And with you," Adaire said, to Solange

Solange asked, "Do you think so? I don't know what to think about that. I don't know enough about Faerie politics to have an opinion. But he's such a good painter. And poor Spike."

So, Adaire must have gone to visit the dragons, Tuuli decided.

The hall was growing more and more crowded. People waiting for the celebration to begin.

Adaire had finished eating. She got up and took both Tuuli's, and her own, dirty plates to a nearby kitchen cart loaded with dirty dishes. Then she sat down again and sipped her May wine.

Tuuli could see through the windows that outside, the sun had set. In the courtyard, wood was being piled up in preparation for the celebrations. Fires would be lit all over. Beltane was a fire festival, after all. Celebrating the coming heat of summer, the return of the sun. The fire of birth.

And the fire of sensuality.

Tuuli smiled at Adaire, who was staring at her.

"You realize," said Adaire, "that Beltane isn't the best time to begin a serious relationship."

"Well, then we can have a dalliance until Lammas. Then begin a serious relationship."

Adaire laughed and covered Tuuli's hand with her own. A current of thrilling energy traveled through Tuuli's entire body.

People began leaving the throne room to go outside once the fires were lit.

The sound of thunder signaled the arrival of dragons.

By the time Adaire and Tuuli got outside, the dragons were helping to start the fires and fanning the flames with their wings. Tuuli spotted Keirosum by one fire and grabbed Adaire's hand, dragging her off in that direction.

Keirosum said, "Well, blessed summer to both of you."

"Blessed summer to you," she and Adaire said together.

"How are the hatchlings?" asked Tuuli.

"Growing quickly and always in trouble," said Keirosum. "Tomorrow we will begin teaching the younger ones how to fly."

"So soon?" asked Tuuli.

"If we waited, then they would fall off the edge of the cave to the rocks below. Our young fly early."

Tuuli couldn't remember when she began to fly. But not days after birth. It had been at least two seasons.

"I am sorry," he said. "I did not mean to bring up a painful subject."

"Oh Keirosum, if I got upset every time someone mentioned flying, I would be sad all the time. There is no need to apologize."

Adaire put her arm around Tuuli's waist and pulled her closer.

"I am fine. Really," Tuuli assured both of them. And she was.

A dais had formed from large blocks of marble. The elders climbed on top of it. They had all changed into ornate robes.

Meredith stood in front, her robe made of stiff, probably waterproof, material in blues and greens.

"Welcome," she said, in a loud voice which carried over the swelling crowd. "Merry summer to you all!"

The Fae roared back, "Merry summer!"

Brian moved forward. He wore light, loose grass-green pants tied with a drawstring and a vest the color of dried barley.

Standing at his feet stood Rowan.

"We have some distressing news. Some of the Fomorians' offspring have Fae magic. And they are using it as a weapon. This beautiful fox is not truly a fox. She is Fae. She left Faerie when it was open and was caught by some of them. They transformed her into a fox. It has taken her some time to return home. Her mind was altered during the transformation and for a long time, she couldn't remember who she was."

The elders formed a circle around the vixen, who stood in the center. Tuuli watched as they combined their power. Energy swirled around them like colored smoke. Even from halfway across the courtyard, Tuuli could feel the surge of their powerful magic.

The energy surrounded the fox and she yipped. In surprise? Or pain? Tendrils of the magic nudged at her form as if trying to move inside her.

Parts of the fox's body shimmered into another form and back to fox again. Tuuli glimpsed a Fae foot before it turned to fox again. A Fae nose, then fox.

Three nearby dragons, Attania, Goshania and Silver, sent

out their energy to join with that of the Fae. Their energy looked more like rainbow colored streams of sunlight.

Together their magic made the fox's form turn into Fae and hold the changes. She was an elder. An earth spirit, tall and strong. With golden blond and silver hair down to her ankles. And skin the color of dried fall grass. Her copper color eyes gleamed in the fire and torchlight.

Several Fae in the crowd gasped.

Someone called out, "Lea!"

The earth spirit looked at the Fae who'd spoken, her face wrinkled as if in confusion.

"Lea," said Brian.

The earth spirit looked down at her hands, as if just now realizing she'd been turned back into herself and was no longer a fox. Tears streamed down her face.

Aura embraced her and led her towards the steps. Two healers helped her down and took her to the edge of the crowd to tend to her.

Ogden, who wore loose brown pants and a soft green shirt the color of new leaves, said, "This is what some of the Fomorian offspring can do. They have the magic of both their parents, Fae, and Fomorian. And right now their allegiance is to the Fomorians. We have ourselves to blame for not making them feel at home in Faerie."

Conley stood next to him. He wore a hard leather and brass skirt, like Roman warriors had once worn. His arms were crossed.

"We cannot allow this to happen again," he said.

Aura moved to the front. Her robes were purple, blue and silver. Made of a gauzy material which floated as she walked. Her large wings unfolded behind her.

"We believe Lea will be fine. It may take some time before she comes back to herself." Aura paused.

She was pointedly watching the healers escort Lea into the palace. They were followed by several Fae, who apparently had known her.

Aura continued, "We think we have found a solution to our problems with the Fomorians. We will not speak of it here. We will test our theory and then announce its success."

Meredith came forward to join her.

"And once again we would like to wish you a blessed Beltane. Summer is come. For tonight, at least, enjoy the ease of summer. We celebrate as our ancestors always have."

The elders bowed elaborately to the crowd and left the dais. Someone in the crowd began to fiddle a reel. They were joined by a drum, keeping the beat. A flute trilled through the air.

The crowd cleared the center of the courtyard and dancers filled it.

Tuuli pulled Adaire into the center and they joined in the dance, Adaire laughing.

At least for tonight, life was good. She had found love again. That gave her the strength to face anything.

And there was hope for the morrow.

Both Sides Dig In …
The Fae struggle to win the war against the Fomorians as a cold, dark winter descends upon Faerie.
The Council of Luminaries tries a new tactic, mead pacified the Fomorians once. Their experiment triggers an astonishing chain of events.

The fate of Faerie hangs in the balance. What can the Fae do to make victory tip in their direction?

The fifth and final book of this richly imagined and visionary series takes us on a wild ride that surprises, and wraps the ending of the series perfectly.

The Bones of the Earth: Book 5

FAERIE CONFLUENCE: THE BONES OF THE EARTH, BOOK 5

FAERIE CONFLUENCE: THE BONES OF THE EARTH, BOOK 5 - CHAPTER 1 - FIACHNA

Fiachna crouched deep in the meadow grass. The broken and bleached strands provided scant cover, only coming up to his chest. His sword sheath scraped on the limestone, which the grass grew up out of. He could feel Egan's hot breath on his back.

His mouth felt dry. Picking up a small broken piece of stone, he stuck it it his mouth. That helped. And not just because he was stone Fae.

Liquid trickled down his cheek. He wiped it off with the back of his hand and saw blood. He'd been hit by flying debris coming from the Fomorians' huge winds. The wound would heal, but leave a mark. He had never been among the best looking Fae. He hoped Clare wouldn't mind the scar.

His leather pants, boots, wool shirt and cloak were soaked through. His waist-length gray and brown hair was tied back. Driving rain streamed down his face. He ignored the discomfort. After spending millennia walking the boundaries of Faerie, this was nothing.

They hid downwind of the Fomorians. Watching and waiting. Crouched outside the boundary of Faerie.

The giants stank of rotted meat and their own filth. It had been at least a month since they'd been released from the vault and even the near constant rain hadn't improved their smell.

The Fomorians had gathered with their offspring on the north side of Faerie. Fiachna couldn't actually see many of the winds, just their effect on the trees bordering the other side of the meadow. He felt freezing cold on his left, that must be Conand of the north wind. Humid heat on his right, might have been Hurricane. Surely, Domnu of the deep abyss of the ocean, wasn't there. She rarely came on land. Fiachna couldn't be sure who else was missing.

He certainly didn't underestimate them. They'd battled the Fae and dragons to a standstill. The Fomorians might be fewer, but Faerie still hadn't found a way to match their power.

He shifted his weight gradually, trying again to accurately count the moving enemy. So far the count was thirty-nine. He didn't recognize all of them.

Domnu, the Mother of them all, that great all-encompassing wave of ocean, scared him the most. He didn't see her and hoped she'd grown weary and gone home. Back to the depths.

Fiachna saw Cethlenn who resembled a flowing white vapor, like the fog she controlled. Corb of the sea, his watery body moving fluidly across the land. Conand of the north wind, taking the shape of a whirling gray and white mass. Elatha the great huntress, looking fierce with a necklace of bones. Dela, whose power he couldn't discern, but whose strong potent force was palpable.

Most of the Fomorians were always shifting. Continuously

moving from a form that had two legs, two arms, a torso and a head, then back into their elemental body. Each one of those different from any other.

The rest of the Fomorians were offspring. Àed, the volcano, gray with red smoking depths. Muir of the deep black sea, with a body that couldn't seem to hold a shape. Ùisdean of the stone islands, with a gray angular body that even Fiachna of the stone people wouldn't want to go up against. There were also Fomorians whose powers looked like sea monsters, lightening and blizzards. Another one, so deep a black it looked like a hole in the world, stood off to the side. Saying nothing and not interacting with the others. That one had an ominous presence which set Fiachna on edge. Plague was the only name that came to mind.

Balor, the King of the Fomorians, sat on a boulder the size of a huge auroch. The giant was about twelve feet tall. Bellowing at all the others. His power was the ravage of drought. He had a third eye in the middle of his forehead which he'd covered with several pieces of cloth, one layered over the other, and tied in back. His baleful eye was a weapon that Fiachna hoped never to see again. He was one of the few Fomorians who Fiachna had never seen change form.

Balor stood up, looking at something near the boundary of Faerie.

Fiachna straightened up a bit, following the giant's gaze.

A cart was coming out of Faerie. Being pulled by a horse and accompanied by two Fae. Fiachna could feel the intense magic surrounding the cart.

Balor walked across the meadow towards it, the others following.

At their approach the illusionary Fae shrieked and ran back

into Faerie. The horse, also not real, broke loose of its harness and headed back to Faerie as well. The magic was there for the Fomorian's benefit. Fiachna hoped they couldn't see through it.

The cart sat there, loaded down with bottles of mead as if on its way to a human village. As if it was normal for Fae to trade with humans.

"It's a trick," said Conand, as Balor picked up one of the bottles and uncorked it. The bottle looked like a child's glass in an adult's hand.

"Taste it," roared Balor, holding the bottle out.

The offspring exchanged glances, as if they didn't want to obey and were waiting for one of the others to go first. Finally Muir, of the deep black sea, took it and sipped it.

"Take a big drink," said Balor.

Muir did. He handed the bottle back to Balor.

"What is it?" asked Elatha.

"It's mead."

"It has to be a trick. If it's not poisoned, then it must be enchanted," said Conand.

They all stared at the bottles and then at Muir, who was still licking his lips lips and smiling.

Nothing happened.

Then the all black one, Plague, spotted Fiachna and Egan.

Plague yelled, pointing with his arm, hand and finger, creating a dark line across the land.

Fiachna created a spell of confusion, and twisting, threw himself over Egan. He shifted completely into his element, earth. Turning into a large rock. Hard, whitish gray with moss attached in places.

He breathed heavily, shooting up a spell that might hide all the magic circling around them. Egan didn't move, just lay there, shutting his fire down.

Fiachna felt the ground shaking beneath him as the Fomorians came closer.

"What is it?"

"It's just a bloody rock," said Balor, kicking Fiachna in the ribs.

He didn't flinch, although pain shot through him.

"I saw something, I tell you," said Plague. "And it weren't no rock."

"Well I don't think the fucking Faeries can turn into boulders. Can they?" asked Corb.

"Nah," said one of the others, whose voice Fiachna didn't recognize.

"I wouldn't be so sure," said Dela. "They're tricky bastards those Fae."

"It's a rock," said Balor. "I hate this place."

"Gives me the creeps," said another.

"Let's leave," said a deeper voice.

"No!" roared Balor. "We leave when I say so. We get our revenge first."

"Then let's go drink some mead," said Plague.

Cethlenn said, "It's a trick. We can't eat or drink anything connected with Faerie."

"Then what good is it for us to knock all their walls down and take over? When we conquer it and can't eat or drink nuthin' then it's pointless," said a whiny voice.

"We conquer them, kill them all and destroy Faerie. Then we can leave," said Balor, as if tired of all the arguing.

Fiachna's belly felt far too warm. Egan wasn't holding his fire in well enough. If he didn't cool off Fiachna would begin to melt. He felt the spell keeping the magic invisible begin to waver. He was tired. Fiachna refocused his concentration.

"Let's try another area," said Dela. "Maybe their defenses aren't so strong where they haven't already been fighting."

The vibrations of their footsteps diminished into the distance.

Fiachna created a glamour that would disguise them and let go of the rock spell. A wave of fatigue ran through him as he opened his eyes. He couldn't see anyone, but the stink of Fomorians hung in the air. Was one of them hiding nearby?

He sent to Egan, *'I think there's still one here. Stay still.'*

They didn't move for a very long time. And even then, Fiachna kept the glamour of the large boulder lying in the middle of the meadow. As he and Egan melted back through the boundary of Faerie, Fiachna saw Plague standing at the other edge of the meadow, blending in with the dark tree trunks.

His eyes were glued to the boulder. Still watching.

Fomorians usually weren't that patient. This one they would need to be careful of.

Fiachna stood inside the transparent boundary, still invisible, keeping the glamour of the stone present.

Plague finally moved after the sun lowered behind the trees. In the growing dusk, Fiachna watched him move across the meadow and touch the stone. The Fomorian realized it wasn't real and stomped where the stone would have been.

Then Plague walked across the meadow to the boundary. He hit it and bounced backwards, repelled by the magic, unable to pass. The Fomorian tried to move very slowly through it, but the boundary pushed back, not allowing him in. He hit it hard and the boundary became as a thick metal wall. Impassable.

Fiachna used his magic to remain invisible and he could see through the boundary.

The Plague seemed more intelligent than most of the other Fomorians. One of the offspring, half Fomorian, half Fae. He should be watched carefully.

Finally, the Plague must have decided it was not worth his time. He turned and ran slowly off towards the east, following the others.

Fiachna let go of his invisibility once the giant was out of sight. Someone should probably go get the cart of mead.

But he turned and headed back to the palace. Let them decide what to do.

He felt tired, unused to doing this kind of magic for such a long time.

He was tired of war.

Fiachna just wanted to return to Glastonbury.

And Clare.

* * *

To continue reading, please buy Faerie Confluence

FAERIE CONFLUENCE: THE BONES OF THE EARTH, BOOK 5

ABOUT THE AUTHOR

Linda Jordan writes fascinating characters, visionary worlds, and imaginative fiction. She creates both long and short fiction, serious and silly. She believes in the power of healing and transformation, and many of her stories follow those themes.

In a previous lifetime, Linda coordinated the Clarion West Writers' Workshop as well as the Reading Series. She spent four years as Chair of the Board of Directors during Clarion West's formative period. She's also worked as a travel agent, a baker, and a pond plant/fish sales person, you know, the sort of things one does as a writer.

Currently, she's the Programming Director for the Writers Cooperative of the Pacific Northwest.

Linda now lives in the rainy wilds of Washington state with her husband, daughter, four cats, a cluster of Koi and an infinite number of slugs and snails.

Her other work includes:
~*Faerie Confluence: The Bones of the Earth, Book 5*
~*Islands of Seattle Series:*
Rescue Mission: Book 1
Explosive Resistance: Book 2
Battle Magic: Book 3
Warriors Rising: Book 4
Divine War: Book 5

~The Jeweled Worlds Series:
Book 1: The Black Opal
Book 2: The Enigmatic Pearl
Book 3: The Flaming Ruby
~Notes on the Moon People
~Falling Into Flight
~Living in the Lower Chakras
All her work can be found at your favorite online bookseller.

Get a FREE ebook!
Sign up for Linda's Serendipitous Newsletter at her website:
www.LindaJordan.net

Visit her at: www.LindaJordan.net
She can be found on Facebook at:
www.facebook.com/LindaJordanWriter
Metamorphosis Press website is at: www.
MetamorphosisPress.com
Goodreads: https://www.goodreads.com/author/show/
2021274.Linda_Jordan

Writers love reviews, even short, simple ones and honest reviews help other readers find the book. Please go to where you bought this book, or Goodreads, and leave a review. It would be much appreciated.